REVIEWS
for
CLASH OF THE TOTEMS AND THE CATASTROPHE OF CALLISTUS
by Yonnie Garber

The Wishing Shelf loved this book so much
we awarded it 5 STARS!

"A fast-paced, skilfully plotted fantasy adventure.
Highly recommended!"
THE WISHING SHELF

"A dramatic end to an ecology focused
coming-of-age duology. Fans of the first book
will really enjoy the sequel."
LOVEREADING4KIDS

CLASH OF THE TOTEMS AND THE CATASTROPHE OF CALLISTUS

BOOK 2

Yonnie Garber

Matador
Unit E2 Airfield Business Park,
Harrison Road, Market Harborough,
Leicestershire. LE16 7UL
Tel: 0116 2792299
Email: books@troubador.co.uk
Web: www.troubador.co.uk/matador
Twitter: @matadorbooks

ISBN 978 1803134 840

British Library Cataloguing in Publication Data.
A catalogue record for this book is available from the British Library.

Printed and bound by CPI Group (UK) Ltd, Croydon, CR0 4YY
Typeset in 11pt Baskerville by Troubador Publishing Ltd, Leicester, UK

Matador is an imprint of Troubador Publishing Ltd

For Dan, Seb, Todd, Bo and Archie,
who take on the world with their relentless
sense of humour.

And to Moo, Poo and Cookie,
who strengthen my resolve with their
unconditional support.

CONTENTS

1

A FIERY START

It was late. My bedroom was so still, so unnervingly quiet. Even the tick-tock of Mum's antique grandfather clock in the hall seemed quieter than usual. I didn't want to sleep despite being struck by an overwhelming tiredness. I tried to fight it. I didn't want to have that awful dream again.

It came to me a few weeks ago, just after I'd overheard Myerscough talking to Mum about Nash. Saxon Nash – the terrifying former head of the Magaecian Circle. Loved by some, hated by many, but feared by all. Every time I mentioned his name, both parents changed the subject. Probably Myerscough's idea. Hendrick Myerscough had manoeuvred his way into our lives with outstanding ease. My *long-lost dad* now lived with us, but calling him "Dad" just didn't come naturally to me. It was lovely to see Mum so happy, although some of the subtle kissing and cuddling they tried to sneak past me was enough to make me gag at times. I almost preferred the moody, depressed Myerscough. Being affectionate and sweet didn't suit him at all. I'd only known him for a year, during which time, I can't deny it, he saved my life. I was grateful, of course, but that didn't excuse him for being absent for the thirteen years of my life that took place before it. He put up with me calling him Hendrick or Myerscough and was obviously making a huge effort to do *Dad* things over the summer, spending time with me, teaching me Magaecian lore, even though I'd rather have spent it doing *Mum* stuff. I missed having time alone with Mum, reading the new magazines she'd get sent for the school library, and baking bread together.

Although it wasn't official, I knew deep down that Saxon Nash was back. Magaecians gossiped a lot. The most irritating piece of gossip I'd heard was that *the newly turned teenager, Ellery Burgess-Myerscough was going to bring back balance to Mother Earth*. Yeah, right! How exactly I was meant to do that was anyone's guess…and I wasn't a newly turned teenager; I was going to be fourteen at the end of the month. People just expected me to share the wisdom and brilliance of my uncle, Darwin Burgess, who was probably the greatest ever leader of the Magaecian Circle. I'd never met him – he died in a car accident before I was born, although, everyone knew that his "accident" was most likely engineered by his successor, Saxon Nash. A sense of foreboding had grasped me so tightly of late, it was suffocating.

An owl hooted outside, which startled me from my troubled thoughts of impending gloom. I sat up in my bed, fidgeting with my fingers, unconsciously biting at a fingernail as I glanced through the window where the curtains didn't meet. I stared until my eyes grew heavy, hypnotised by moving shadows thrown from flickering street lights. I knew I'd have no choice but to surrender to sleep – it would inevitably envelop me, but I was still going to try my darnedest to keep awake as long as possible. It was such a disturbing dream and just so vivid. I probably should have told my mum or Myerscough about it. Perhaps it meant something. Of course, there was also the possibility that perhaps it didn't, and the truth was that I was actually going mad. I tried to calm myself. I thought about my friends; I'd see them again soon when school started in a couple of days. I had some great friends at my new school. It was a school for Magaecians, which wasn't, to my great disappointment, a school for learning magic, but instead a school for kids who respected their planet, Magae – also known as Mother Earth. Magaecians thought that Magae was a living entity capable of doing everything in her power to stay alive. So if humans continued to pollute, damage and destroy her, she would have no option but to destroy us first. That's why Saxon Nash hated Dwellers, the non-Magaecian folk. He thought the only way to save his people was to kill all the Dwellers. Charming man! Thinking about Nash sent my heart into uncomfortable palpitations. I was never going to get to sleep with him on my mind.

I took a couple of deep breaths and began again. I tried reciting the alphabet backwards, hoping to keep my mind off bad thoughts, but I only got as far as "R" before I'd concluded that it took too much effort. I decided that I was overthinking this. All I needed to do was to analyse my dream and to take something positive from it. This wouldn't be difficult:

I only had to ask myself what it was about my dream that frightened me, then try to rationalise my fear. But there were so many things about it that frightened me. It would always start in the same way. I'd try to connect to my honey badger but then, I'd be overwhelmed with distress when my animal totem wasn't there; no matter how hard I tried, I couldn't find it. My brain would scream *danger* like a flashing red sign in my head, causing my senses to jump to high alert. Instead of finding my honey badger, I'd see a hideous creature looming above me, filling me with a dreadful panic that overflowed into my limbs so that they stiffened, rooted to the spot, like a rabbit caught in the headlights of a car. This creature's ivory blades of teeth would drip strings of smelly saliva onto my head and shoulders. An enormous reptile, so much bigger than I was. Some kind of flying serpent king letting out a flaming roar.

I shook my head to remove the vision from my thoughts, which might as well have been tattooed onto the inside of my eyelids as I seemed to see it every time I closed my eyes these days. I shuddered, pulling my bed covers over my shoulders and up to my neck for comfort.

I brought my knees to my chest and hugged them, trying my best to think "happy thoughts" before I fell asleep, but this was proving a lot harder than I'd expected. As I tried far too hard not to think about my disturbing dream, it suddenly dawned on me: a fire-breathing reptile – *that's a dragon!*

"Dragons don't exist," I told myself over and over. *Dragons don't exist.* Perhaps in my head, where I could shapeshift into my totem, maybe here they did. But was I even shapeshifting at all? This was nothing but a nasty dream that I could wake up from – a nightmare, not real but in my head. I was being ridiculous. I released my knees and uncurled my body to lie down, sinking my head onto my soft pillow. It wasn't long before I fell into a deep sleep…

…A moving mountain of scales with glistening talons, sharp as kitchen knives, was ready to slice me to death in a heartbeat. Bulging reptilian eyes so cold, concrete-grey, apart from the long black line of its pupils, traversing through the middle. As smoke poured from its nostrils, sulphur filled the air. I began to choke and became light-headed as I held my breath. The beast roared full throttle, causing my eardrums to throb in protest. The ground beneath me juddered so violently, I lost my footing and crashed to the floor, smashing onto my face, nose first. I blacked out for a minute but when I came to, I recognised my surroundings. I was in my cave, and yet it wasn't my cave, my safe haven – it was different somehow. A strange painted emblem permeated the walls which were desecrated and defiled by this horrible creature. My body ached as I shook from head to foot. The cave that should have been still and calm encased me in fear as I strained to find my way to freedom. Hot monster breath blasted over me and I felt my insides melting. Gasping and gulping, I came face to face with the open jaws of eternal blackness, hovering over me to snap me up and swig me down a terrifying slide, a gullet of doom to my end.

I edged backwards, looking for the way out but there wasn't one. The only way to safety was forwards. I scrambled to my feet, heading for an area of light ahead, hoping it might lead me outside and onto the safe meadow.

The faster I ran, the more I stumbled over my feet. It didn't take me to the outside, to the fresh green grass I longed for, but to a rocky ledge. I knew I shouldn't have looked over it but I did. I wish I hadn't as I was confronted with a void so vast, an endless vacuum of death, it caused my legs to give way. There was nowhere to run. Nowhere to hide. If I didn't jump, I'd be dragon food, for sure. If I did, I'd be splattered human smoothie, and that's if I ever even reached the bottom. I might end up falling forever. A huge wave of adrenaline passed over me. I was supposed to be a honey badger, for goodness' sake. My schoolmate, Nyle Pinkerton, said it was the toughest, coolest, kick-ass totem – so why had it abandoned me? My totem wasn't coming. It wasn't coming. I made my decision fast – human smoothie. I squeezed my eyes shut and jumped, falling so far, for so long before jolting every part of my body on reaching the bottom…

"Ellery! Are you up? It's late. We need to get going. Hurry up!" screamed Mum.

I opened my eyes, sweating with a sense of dread. I was back in my bedroom. I was alive – of course I was alive; it was a dream, it wasn't real. I looked down at my bed sheets which were covered in blood! In fact, there was blood everywhere. I screamed until my voice was hoarse. Mum and Myerscough flung open the door, rushing to my side like a couple of superheroes, only without the capes.

"What's happened?" shrieked my mum, a couple of octaves higher than usual as she examined me for wounds.

Shaking, I couldn't speak.

"You've had a nosebleed," grumbled Myerscough. "You could've gone to the bathroom instead of traipsing blood all round your room, Ellery."

"Sorry," I croaked, touching my nose which felt crusty and horrible. I didn't say any more than that; a dragon, if that's what it was – and I'm *sure* that's what it was, wasn't something a teenager would want to admit to. It was right up there with unicorns, fairies, the Easter Bunny and sparkles. I was too old for that kind of stuff.

"Don't worry, sweetheart," said Mum with a smile. "Go and get washed and dressed. It's late. We're going to the Mitchells' for lunch." She slid off my bedding and took it downstairs to wash.

Hakan and Laura Mitchell were both teachers at my school. They'd been away for most of the year in Alaska, where they had family, so my parents were looking forward to catching up with them. Their kids, Mika and Ashkii, were going to be there too but I didn't know them very well. In fact, I'd always thought Ashkii was a girl, not a boy. I swear I heard Myerscough ask Mitchell last year how Laura and *the girls* were. Mind you, Myerscough was not the type of person to put much effort or importance into finding out anything about any of his friends' kids; too busy with other stuff, like telling people off or arranging meetings with the new Magaecian Circle. And, Mitchell would have been far too polite to have corrected him. Anyway, unlike my parents, I was anything but keen to get going to the Mitchells' for lunch; it was going to be ultra-boring. I stomped down the stairs, stopping halfway, anticipating a sharp pain to stab me in the ribs but it never came. I broke several ribs after my encounter with Saxon Nash last Christmas but that was nearly nine months ago now.

"What are you wearing?" growled Mum. "Let me iron that."

"It's fine," said Myerscough with a wink, but Mum stood rigid with her arm outstretched to receive my creased-up shirt.

"I'll start up the car while you do that," said Myerscough, quickly turning on his heels to avoid seeing his teenage daughter in her bra, which was hardly worth the effort – my boobs were practically non-existent.

Although Myerscough's disposition had improved over the year, I still found him pretty frightening. His voice was deep and gruff, like a wolf with a migraine, not to mention the muscular build that went with it – his hands alone were the size of extra-large pizzas.

We arrived at the Mitchells' in Dormly Village, my freshly pressed shirt feeling as though Mum might have put the hanger back into it somewhere. The village of Dormly was even more rural than Tribourne. I think there was only one other house besides the Mitchells' and that belonged to an old, retired artist that no one had seen in years. Mum wondered if anyone ever checked on him. *"He could be dead in there and no one would ever know."*

As we approached, there were two large canvas tepees in the front garden all covered in hawks, painted on like tattoos. Behind them was a small dwelling, a bungalow which I guessed housed their kitchen and a couple of other rooms, hopefully a toilet at least.

"Hau!" said Mitchell as he walked towards us.

8

"Hau!" returned Myerscough.

Mitchell pulled him into his chest and whispered something into his ear but I couldn't hear what it was.

"Welcome, Nell and Ellery," panted Laura, who ran up the path to greet us. She was always smiling as if every moment was a joy to her. "This is Mika."

I *knew* it was Mika – who else could it have been? I suppose we'd never really been formally introduced so I just smiled politely. Mika was a small, pretty girl with short, black, shiny pigtails and a dark-skinned face that contrasted her unusually light blue eyes.

"Mika starts at Quinton tomorrow," added Laura. "Looking forward to getting back to school, Ellery?"

I nodded with a fake smile. It was a stupid question. I'd much rather be on my summer break than at school, although I suppose I was looking forward to seeing my friends again. I'd not seen them much over the summer as Myerscough wanted to spend time with me...or something like that. My thoughts were interrupted by the vision of a younger, leaner, taller version of Mr Mitchell: sixteen-year-old Ashkii Mitchell. His glossy black hair was scrapped back like silk into a ponytail held by coloured rope. He had brown eyes, and yet when they caught the light they were more like orange. If my friend Letty caught sight of him, she'd probably faint on the spot. She had a serious crush on Mr Mitchell, but Ashkii might well replace that. He shook hands with Myerscough, trying to appear like one of the men but he failed miserably as he tripped over while walking indoors. I think he caught me giggling as I bit my lips together in an attempt to cover it up.

A large tribal feather dreamcatcher hung over the front door, the sparkly beads woven into the web, producing a beautiful pattern on the porch as the sunlight caught them. As I headed inside, a strong smell of cedar filled the air. I couldn't decide if I liked it or not. Walking further in, the walls were strewn with brightly coloured woven rugs, all with geometric patterns of red, yellow and orange. A big circular table filled practically the whole dining room, which was warm and welcoming. The smell of cedar had been replaced with the delicious aroma of cornbread and bean stew, which was served inside the shells of three enormous pumpkins. Luckily the table had sturdy legs; the pumpkins looked so heavy. A selection of mismatched crockery accompanied the cutlery for us to tuck in straight away.

We ate loads and chatted politely about nothing really.

"Ash and Mika, why don't you take Ellery out to show her your tepee? I don't suppose she's been in one before," said Mr Mitchell, looking across to his wife as if to signal something.

"Yes," replied Mrs Mitchell. "Good idea. Nell can help me sort out dessert. I'll get Dad to call you when it's ready."

Ash puffed, blinking in slow motion. "Mika can take her. She doesn't need me."

"Ashkii! Do as your mother asks," snapped Mitchell.

Ash's cheeks reddened and his shoulders dropped. He went ranting on about something or other under his breath then drove his chair back with a loud scrape as he stood, almost toppling it over. He signalled with his head for me and Mika to follow as he stomped outside.

"I don't need a babysitter, thanks," I muttered. "What don't they want us to hear anyway? It can only be boring stuff about the Magaecian Circle."

"Or secret stuff about Nash," whispered Mika.

"Like what?" I said.

"That's the whole point," barked Ash, his American accent far more noticeable now that his mood had changed. "They don't want you to hear. It's not your concern. It's an adult conversation which I should be hearing and probably would be if you weren't round for lunch."

"If I'm old enough to face Nash and fight him, then I'm old enough to hear what they're saying about him," I retorted indignantly, putting my hands into my trouser pockets to hide my trembling fingers at the very mention of Nash's name. Unfortunately, Nash and I had something in common. We were both ebonoid, which meant that we had the ability to produce negative energy physically. Although it sounded really cool, it was actually a curse. When I became angry there was always the possibility I could inadvertently hurt someone – *really* hurt someone that was close to me. There was also the added bonus that if I used my negative power too much, I would become like Nash: out of control, cruel with harmful intent and I would lose myself to the grave darkness and ruin on my downward slope to self-destruction. Ebonoid didn't have a great record of survival through history. I'd been told time and again by my teachers to control my temper but this was an enormous task for a teenager, and they knew it. One teacher even commented that temper and teenager went together like salt and pepper. In my case it seemed to be more thunder and lightning.

Ash looked at his sister, then nodded. "Follow me, then," he said. He took us round the back of the bungalow where there was a small drainpipe sticking out. He put his finger to his lips before unscrewing the bottom of the pipe very slowly and quietly. As if by magic, both our fathers' voices were as clear as crystal, carried up to us as if we'd put an intercom system in place.

"Mika discovered it," said Ash.

We each lay on our stomachs and listened to the clink of ice cubes in whisky glasses from inside...or it might have been brandy. I didn't know what adults drank after dinner, only that it smelled disgusting.

"She'll kill us all, Hendrick," said Mitchell. "That's why you've got to be proactive. You can't wait any longer, my friend. You've got to take care of this."

"But she's just a child," Myerscough replied.

"She's an ebonoid. You've got to act before she becomes like Nash. You know it will happen. It's inevitable."

"No! It's not!"

"Stop kidding yourself. How do you think she'll react when she finds out you haven't let her out of your sight all summer, too afraid she might hurt her closest friends if she were left alone with them? You can't watch over her forever. It's only a matter of time before something bad happens. I'm sorry – there is no alternative here."

There was an awkward silence apart from my heart, which was banging loudly in my ears. Ash tried to put the pipe back but I flicked his hand away.

"You have to act now, Hendrick...*now*! You know what has to be done."

"I'm just not sure I'll be able to do it."

"You will. You must. You're the only one that can. I'll help you, my friend."

Ash forced the pipe back. "You shouldn't listen to any more. It's out of context."

"Out of context?" I shouted. "Which part? The bit where your father was insinuating that my father should murder me in my bed before term begins; or the part where *dear Daddy* agrees to let your father help him do it?"

"The first part?" replied Mika as if I'd asked a trick question with rainbow points for the correct answer.

Ash rolled his eyes at his sister's response. "Listen, Ellery, our dads have known each other for decades – always on the side of good. They're not murderers, either one."

I didn't answer as I followed Ash and Mika down to the tepees.

"You've got to help me, Ash. I'm not safe. I know you can drive," I said, pulling him by the arm to make him turn and face me.

"I'm underage."

"I'm under siege! Please help me. Just get me to a station. I know where to go from there."

"Where?" he demanded.

"I can't tell you right now. Besides…it's probably safer for you not to know anyway."

He looked anxiously at his sister. "You mustn't tell, Mika. Not a word."

"I promise," she replied, with a nod.

"Dessert, kids!" hollered Mr Mitchell.

"Tell Mum and Dad we're meditating with our totems and we'll be in when we've finished," whispered Ash.

"Coming!" yelled Mika, giving a little signal to wait before she set off back the other way to the bungalow. Within seconds of her leaving, she returned. "Here," she said, throwing the car keys to her brother.

"Good one." Ash smiled. "Dad keeps them in his tepee."

"Won't they hear us start the engine?" I asked, biting off one of my nails.

"Dad's car's electric. No sound," replied Ash.

We sprinted across the grass and to the car, a small silver hatchback. It smelled of tobacco and sweets – not that I was complaining. I'd have sat in it if it smelled of old drains and the rotting body of the *possibly dead* artist up the road if it meant I could get away from those two scheming fathers. Ash reversed like a grown-up and drove expertly away, sweating profusely at the possibility of getting caught, I suspect. He stopped outside Dormly station.

"Now what?" He gestured angrily with both hands open, waiting for me to answer back with an intelligent plan.

"Now you go back and make up a good excuse…like I *made* you take me or something."

"You *did* make me take you, Ellery," he snapped. "Your father will kill me…*my* father will kill me."

"That's why you can't know where I'm going."

"All the more reason for them to kill me. Maybe I should come with you. You're going to need help anyway."

I looked across at my handsome new friend, his stunning eyes staring straight back into mine. I felt my heart begin to dance and my cheeks tingled as they must have turned red. I held them in my hands, embarrassed by the heat they produced. I slid them across my mouth pretending to blow on my fingers to make them warm, even though it was a lovely sunny day. I so wanted Ashkii to be my hero, to protect me from danger but I knew in my heart that he wouldn't have a clue what to do in a crisis. It might also be dangerous for him if everyone was trying to kill me, in which case, perhaps I was being selfish. I was so confused. Why would Myerscough suddenly turn against me? I thought I was meant to be the one to finish what my uncle had started and bring back balance to Magae.

"No," I began, opening the car door to get out. "You go back. It'll give me a bit more time." As I turned to leave him, I suddenly remembered I had no money on me. I quickly knocked on the passenger window to ask Ash to lend me some cash before he pulled away. The glass shattered with a crisp crunch. A jigsaw of a hundred glass pieces fell out like loose teeth.

"Why did you bang it so hard? My dad's gonna kill me."

"Again?" I answered sarcastically, knowing full well that a little tap on the window wasn't the reason it broke. It must've been faulty, a small unnoticed crack somewhere. "He can't kill you twice, Ash."

"Here," he barked, grabbing a handful of pound coins stashed down the cup holder of his dad's car before practically throwing them through the broken window. His teeth were so tightly clenched there might have been invisible wires holding his jaws together. He drove off, the car's back wheels shooting up dust and stones as he did.

I needed to think. Where could I go? Who could I stay with? Not Thomas or Letty, that would be far too close to home and Myerscough would find me immediately. Then there was Dave, of course – Daveena Rupasinghe – the Magaecian guru who helped me last year…but that would be an obvious place too. I stood looking up at the station timetable screen for ideas. Where else could I go in London? Quinton House? My old headmistress, Mrs Huckabee, would be there. I could trust Mrs Huckabee. She'd know what to do. She wasn't headmistress any more, she was the new head of the Magaecian Circle. As I pondered, I felt my stomach knotting but it relaxed temporarily when I noticed an exasperated mum scolding her little girl for getting her lollipop stuck in her hair. The little girl screamed spasmodically as her mum tried to unstick the dark red sweet from her tangled strands. I turned away, not wanting her to see me smirking. As I did, I caught a waft of mint growing wildly on the green station bank. I clambered up to pick a few leaves and caught the stream gurgling on the other side. Mint always reminded me of home; of Mum's cooking; of the mint tea she always drank; and of Lionel, my dog whose nose always smelled of mint from rummaging in the mint bush in our garden. My heart felt suddenly heavy at the thought of leaving all that behind. I placed the leaves in my trouser pocket, next to my totem stone which I always carried with me.

It was a slippery descent as I slid down to the platform towards a stern-looking, middle-aged man, whose stride hastened to a gallop in order to avoid me. He wore a smart camel coat which covered a dark suit beneath it. He took out a black shiny pipe and filled it with tobacco. I'd never seen anyone smoke a pipe before – apart from Sherlock Holmes in films – and was intrigued. His brown, bushy eyebrows jumped up and down as he inhaled the flame at the end of his matchstick. As I bit off another fingernail, I stared, almost hypnotised by the flame dancing in and out of his pipe. A small spark separated and removed itself, flying into the man's hair, singeing off the middle part of one of his eyebrows in the process. The man squealed and dropped his pipe as he smacked his head to put out the flames which seemed only to make matters worse.

"That man's head's exploding!" shrieked the little girl, pointing. Her mother wasn't listening, totally oblivious, still trying to remove the lollipop.

The poor man became increasingly unsteady on his feet, hands outstretched hysterically, part of his hair alive, still ignited, a streak of orange running through it. I raced to help him but he slipped and fell before I'd even got close. He landed hard on his back against a recycling bin which went up like a Roman candle. I tore off my hoodie and threw it over him which seemed to do the job – but a wave of flames had already spread along the platform. Sparks rained quickly through the air before joining together to create an erratic flaming whirlwind which engulfed several newspaper stands. I looked across to the man who was no longer alight despite the fact that the rest of the place was fast combusting as Dormly station suddenly acquired an eternal flame in the middle of it.

Alarm bells screeched, station staff appearing from everywhere, attempting to put out the fire, brandishing shiny red extinguishers which looked as though they'd never been used before. Thick smoke belched from the platform, the acrid flavour filling my nostrils. It seemed to be getting out of hand unnervingly fast from such a small spark. It didn't make any sense.

"Ellery!"

I turned with a jump to see Hakan frogmarching his son towards me. The pipe-man who'd started the fire was being attended to by a station conductor, examining his lack of eyebrows and singed new fuzzy hairstyle. I thought this might be a good time to leg it. I turned to scarper but was met, head-on by the muscular wall of Myerscough's torso. My heart quickened uncomfortably. I felt it pounding, every beat more unpleasant than the last as the pressure built up to reach my ears, which weren't registering any sound, drowned out by sirens blaring and people screaming.

"Going somewhere, Ellery?" he growled.

The hairs on my arms stood up. I gritted my teeth. I looked back to see Ash being shouted at by his father. Clenching my fists as I turned to Myerscough, I forgot briefly that my ebonoid power was useless on him. He was genetically immune. He grabbed my hands and forced them into a namaste position, then moved aside for me to see an old lady trying to catch her breath on the ground.

"Your handy work, young lady," he began as he pointed to the fallen woman. "And no doubt this whole fiery charade too. Does every new school year have to start with a blazing inferno?"

I said nothing.

"We need to get out of here," shouted Myerscough over the screams of hysterical passengers and staff, running around like headless chickens – some yielding their fire extinguishers out of control to spread long trails of meringue-like foam all over the place; others standing gormlessly, shocked by the turn of events at the usually quiet station. An otherwise mild day had turned into anything but, the temperature rising as flames grew around us, engulfing the antiquated station, pouring out dirty smoke everywhere. Embers spat among the sooty particles floating about, covering the ground in a dusty grey layer.

"All passengers exit the station, please!" screamed a lady over the tannoy in between coughs.

Myerscough grabbed my arm but I swung myself free.

"Go on then!" I screamed, causing passengers to turn momentarily from the chaos in favour of watching our commotion instead. "Kill me! Just get it over with."

"What?" answered Myerscough, furrowing his brow.

"I know you want to kill me."

"I'd love to throttle you right now, young lady, I really would," spat Myerscough. "But unfortunately, fathers are not allowed to kill their children...which is just as well. I can't imagine there'd be many kids left if we could."

"I don't understand. You told Mitchell he needed to help you to kill me."

Myerscough stood in stunned silence before letting out an enormous laugh that filled every platform of the burning station, almost drowning out the sirens of oncoming fire engines. "How the bloody hell did you come to that conclusion?"

"I heard you – both of you. You said, 'She will kill us all. You've got to act before she becomes like Nash'."

Myerscough shook his head, then put his hand on his stubbly chin. His sweaty forehead crinkled as he let out another blast of laughter, so forceful it seemed to fan the flames even more. "You're an idiot!"

"Okay, Hendrick. Not too harsh, my friend," butted in Mitchell as he pushed us both out of the station exit. "Let's get out of here and go for a coffee. There's a cafe just down the road. Should be a safe enough distance away."

I looked over at Ash and tutted. He'd failed big time to be my knight in shining armour. I followed Myerscough and the other two to the smelly local cafe which felt like miles and miles away – definitely not *just down the road*.

"Firstly," began Myerscough, grabbing a menu off the adjacent table, "you shouldn't eavesdrop."

Ash looked down at the grubby table, stained with age-old tomato ketchup and baked bean residue.

"Hakan *did* say that she will kill us all...*she*, meaning Magae, not you. I also agreed to let Hakan help me to teach you through your totem so that you won't become like Nash. He said I am the only one who can do it because I am the only one immune."

A waitress came over with a scrappy piece of paper to take our order of three black coffees. I wanted nothing and just shook my head at her.

"An orange juice for the young lady, please," said Myerscough, which irritated me. However, when it came, I drank it to soothe my throat, which was still burning from the smoke.

"You see, Ellery," said Mitchell softly, "your *gift* will grow as you do, and that will need to be managed closely."

"I know how to manage my *gift*, thank you."

"No, you don't," said Myerscough curtly. "Judging by the state of Dormly station, I'd say you're way out of your depth."

"I didn't start the fire!" I yelled, people glaring at me as if I were some juvenile arsonist intent on destroying their local village. "It was the man with a stupid pipe. I might be an ebonoid but I'm not Captain Fire-fingers!"

Myerscough's face crinkled as if he should have heard of Captain Fire-fingers. Ash, on the other hand, dribbled out a bit of his coffee with a snigger. He caught my eye with a smile but then stared vacantly back at the table, probably still feeling guilty about giving me away within the first five minutes of returning home. I should have found a station further away than Dormly. It was a stupid idea to go from there. The only upside was that at least now I knew that Myerscough and Mitchell weren't going to kill me after all. The downside was that there would be a hell of a punishment coming my way.

2

FINDING THE ANSWERS

School started at the old Tribourne Estate again. Apparently, the council agreed to let us start our term here despite having to share the space with Saint Timothy's pupils, whose school had never recovered. It was still a pile of depressing burned-out rubble. Most of the Saint Timothy's pupils opted to join the school in the next village or were sent to boarding schools up in London after the fire. The rest were forced to use the old Tribourne Hotel rooms as temporary classrooms. None of the remaining pupils wanted to join the Magaecians, so although the Burgess Manifesto was having some effect... it definitely wasn't having enough. A lot more Dweller kids were aware of what a disastrous place the Earth would become if we didn't change things, but it was their parents who didn't really care. It was frustrating. I was beginning to see why Nash felt the way that he did. I stopped myself from continuing with that line of thought. I didn't want to become like him…I couldn't do that.

It was like Piccadilly Circus, a mixture of over-excited students mixed with less-excited teachers. Magaecian kids and Dweller kids facing off against one another. It was a mess. The Dwellers were ushered out of the hall and into another room somewhere by Mrs Hayhurst who was helped by a young Dweller teacher.

"How was your summer?" asked Letty, striding in an ungainly fashion towards me. She'd grown loads over the holidays and towered over me, thin gangly legs like stilts.

"I missed you," I replied. "Myerscough kept me away. He thought I might kill you with my ebonoid powers."

Letty laughed. "That's such nonsense."

"What's such nonsense?" asked Thomas, who had joined us.

Before I had time to answer, a loud *"Silence, please!"* rang round the hall. I looked around to see a few new faces as well as the old ones. Nyle waved from the other side of the room, Kemp and Orford trailing behind him. Orford was almost unrecognisable: a man with a boy's face. His thatch of dark hair resembled a dirty carpet. I'm not sure what look he was going for but he'd severely missed a cool boy-band look, managing instead an impoverished outgrown-his-trousers look.

"Welcome, younglings. I am your new headteacher, Mr Peter Butterly," said the man, tall and upright.

"Did he say his name was Peanut Buttery?" asked Thomas.

I looked over to see Letty's shoulders shuddering as she tried her best to stifle her giggles. This set me off too. Despite trying my utmost to control myself, I let out an explosive snigger, resulting in a heavy prod in the back from Myerscough. I directed my eyes to the new head in an attempt to avoid being sent out of the room with a yellow. The new head had a large, leathery face, not soft and pink like Mrs Huckabee's, but olive and stern. His chin was strong and square, his eyes critical as they scrutinised every pupil in the room.

"I'd like you all to enrich your experience of life this year," began Mr Butterly.

"Boring!" whispered Nyle, who stopped instantly after a nudge from Myerscough.

"I'd like you to use your senses to the full. Instead of bouncing along ignorantly, I'd like you to savour your surroundings. Take more notice of Magae's flowers, trees and rocks. Pay attention to the clouds and sense what may lie ahead."

"What a load of rubbish," added Nyle, receiving yet another nudge in the back.

"I want you to heighten your senses to their full potential. Retrain your brains to see the unseen. Try tree roots as a compass; find south by using the stars; identify hedgehogs hidden in fallen leaves, or snails working their way through decaying matter; re-walk a trail with new knowledge to uncover secrets hidden previously. We are all part of Magae. The air, the soil, the water and all living organisms are part of our flesh. This connection with Magae makes us human as we strive to coexist with her plants and animals."

"Blimey," said Kemp, who'd managed to barge his way through to us. "That's a bit deep and meaningful for a welcome talk."

"I want you to pay attention to your tutors; work hard and create your own extraordinary tales," continued Butterly. He then went on to explain the rainbow system to the Year 8s and the other new students who were listening intensely, probably wishing they'd never come now that they'd discovered their new headteacher was clearly off his trolley.

"And one last thing, students," said Mr Butterly, taking a deep breath as he acquired a second wind. "I've had some disturbing emails from several parents who appear to have reached the conclusion – the *wrong* conclusion, I might add – that having an ebonoid in our midst is not a good thing."

Pupils' heads turned, all eyes glaring at me.

I felt Myerscough edge nearer.

"Ebonoid get their name from the ebony tree which produces a dark black wood. This has nothing to do with dark or black magaec, but is due to the fact that the ebony species is considered as threatened and should be protected...just like ebonoid should be protected. An ebonoid is probably the closest related living being to Magae, and as such, has a purpose to protect her. Mr Nash, misguided though he was, attempted to protect his planet and his people. It was in his make-up to do so. Of course, Magae is unable to distinguish between Dweller and Magaecian. To her, we are all just human beings which is why we must make our Dweller counterparts see that we can only remain on Magae if we change our habits and change them now. *Anything* is better than nothing, and *anything* is a step nearer to a solution. There are still Nash followers who believe the only way forward is to remove the Dwellers, but we all know that we must work together, Dweller and Magaecian alike. So, let's make a difference this year and change, re-educate and unite with our fellow man so that we may all remain on the planet we love. We need to get across the importance of respecting Magae, taking no more than our land supports."

Myerscough nodded in agreement and subtly backed off.

"Please nominate an individual from each class to pick up the timetables for the term from my provisional office. The rest of you please follow your class tutor back to your temporary classrooms."

"I'll do it," I mouthed to Myerscough, who nodded in agreement.

"A couple of announcements before you go," added Butterly. "Make sure all wellington boots are marked clearly with your names. There's been a lot of confusion on previous field trips with pupils wearing odd boots. Also, those taking whistling lessons need to meet with Miss Trollope after assembly, please."

Letty and I were giggling again.

"All those wishing to join tree-hugging club, please see Mr Rivers at break time," added Butterly.

"Do you two want to go out with a yellow?" growled Myerscough.

Letty and I looked down at the floor, biting our lips.

"Lastly," continued Butterly, "all those in their last year of school considering a year out next year to see the world, please speak to Mrs Badger about how you can offset your carbon footprint."

"Mrs Badger? No way!" snorted Letty.

"Out!" Myerscough attempted to whisper through gritted teeth but it came out more like a burp.

"She's got some excellent volunteering schemes like ocean conservation projects, building schools, reforesting tropical rainforests, tree planting and other conservation work." Butterly stopped, clocking Letty leaving the room. He cleared his throat then continued. "Orford Nibley-Soames, come to my office after assembly, please."

I looked over at Orford, who'd gone bright red at having his name read out loud.

"What've you done?" I whispered.

He shrugged.

We left the assembly room in silence and I walked with Orford to Butterly's room. There inside was Mrs Nibley-Soames. She didn't look how I'd remembered her, which was super smart, hair tied back into a neat ponytail. Today she looked grey – not her hair but her skin, and her eyes were all red and bulgy as if she'd not slept in a month. Orford had been living with his grandma for a while. He'd tried to reconcile with his parents after Giftmas but it didn't work out. Giftmas was a Magaecian term, a bit like Christmas but it embraced all religions and races. It was the one time in the year to cherish the gift of life and the chance to bring peace and goodwill to all men, no matter one's beliefs. I think Orford's mum wanted to resolve their family differences and make it work but not his dad. That's what Nyle told me, anyway.

Mrs Nibley-Soames's face crinkled with a smile as she caught sight of Orford's ill-fitting trousers, but she turned her nose up at Orford's normally sleek hair now strongly resembling a dead rat.

"Orford," said Mrs Nibley-Soames, jumping up from her chair to greet her long-lost son.

"The timetables are by the door here," said Mr Butterly, handing me a wad of Year 9 ones. He welcomed Orford into the room to be reunited with his mum, then followed me out to leave Orford alone with her.

I took the timetables back to Myerscough and sat on the floor among my friends.

"Okay, Year 9s...we are starting the term with a chat from Mr Mitchell about your totems...then we'll be making tracks to Quinton House. There, we'll get instructions for our peregrination."

"Where will that be, sir?" asked Delia.

"You'll find out soon enough."

Mr Mitchell entered the room, sending Letty's face on fire with an instant red glow. He was followed in by a couple of Dweller teachers holding pens and paper.

"These teachers are to observe our lesson today. They'll be at the back of the classroom so just concentrate on me and pretend they're not there, please," began Mitchell with a smile as the teachers made themselves comfortable on some chairs at the back, pens at the ready.

Letty nodded conscientiously. Kemp growled under his breath.

"Now, most of you will still have your original totem but as you mature and grow, so your totem may change. Of course, some of you may have more than one and some of you may have a completely different totem that will be with you for just as long as you need it. It will vary from person to person." He looked around the class, checking on our responses.

"Has anyone experienced a change?"

I looked down at my crossed legs on the dusty wooden floor. There was no way I was going to divulge the dragon I saw, so avoiding eye contact with Mitchell was, in my mind, the safest option.

"Okay, kids. Let's find our totems. Don't try to unite with others. I want you to concentrate exclusively on your own. You may still sense others' totems, of course. If you do, that's fine. I'll be instructing you all the way, so there's no need to worry about anything."

I held my totem stone between my palms; a hint of mint lingered on it from the leaves I'd picked at Dormly station the day before. As I closed my eyes, a sinking feeling took over my stomach at what might lie ahead.

"Find your safe chamber and walk through it," began Mitchell, softly. "Exit onto Magae's grassy field and feel her peace run through you so that your totem may enter. Feel your totem's energy and enjoy its company."

I felt the power of my honey badger; its energy, its vitality had returned. I felt calm as I enjoyed its company and so thankful for its presence. I stayed with my totem for quite a while until I heard Mitchell's voice, faint but clear.

"Move slowly back to your safe hideaway and feel relaxed…"

As I moved back towards my cave, I felt an uncomfortable heat. The cave had changed, it wasn't my cave any more and the honey badger was no longer with me. I was alone. Burning fumes entered my nose and caused me to cough. I rubbed my eyes, blurred with the smoke to see only too clearly the one thing I really didn't want to see. I rubbed my eyes again and shook my head to remove the hideous dragon from in front of me – so very real here in my mind – it wasn't budging. Its talons out to stab me, its teeth, like a sharp, rocky landscape ready to puncture me to death before swallowing me whole. I couldn't fight such a large beast alone and I couldn't sense my friends' totems to help me. My only choice was to run for it. I lost my footing and crashed to the floor, head first yet again. I scrambled to my feet. As flames filled the cave, I ran as fast as I possibly could through the unsinged part of the chamber to what I hoped was the entrance. Puffing and panting, I heard the faint voice of my teacher: *"…deep breaths back to the classroom… deep breaths…"*.

I jolted open my eyes, still puffing and panting.

"You okay?" asked Letty, passing me a tissue.

"What's this for?"

She pointed to a crimson pool of blood on the floor in front of me.

"Okay, class. Any questions?"

Delia asked something intelligent, but I'd zoned out, feeling quite shaky and a little bit sick. I loved visiting my totem – at least, I used to. It relaxed me and allowed me to clear my mind somehow. Now it was a total nightmare, not just in my dreams but in my meditation too.

"Let's call it quits for today," said Mitchell. "Go get some snacks for break time, then meet back here to get ready for Quinton House."

As we packed away, Mitchell came towards me and Letty. I could feel her nudging me. I think I could feel her smiling all over, if that was even possible.

"Letty, sweetie, will you please stay with Ellery. I think I should get Dr Wilberforce to take a look at that," he said, putting my hand containing the blood-soaked tissue back to my nose.

"It's fine," I snapped, resulting in a scowl from my teacher. "I mean, it's stopped now…really. Just a silly nosebleed, that's all, sir."

"I'll be back in ten minutes. Stay here, please."

Mitchell signalled to the Dweller teachers to follow him out of the room. Within minutes of their departure, Nyle, Kemp, Thomas and Delia came back through the door. There was a noticeable absence from Orford, missing since assembly.

"What's going on?" asked Thomas, taking a large bite from an apple. He offered it round to everyone but we all refused as his slobbery saliva slipped down the shiny green skin.

"It's nothing," I snapped again. "Just a nosebleed, for goodness' sake."

"Come on. We're your fat friends. What's wrong?" asked Thomas.

I paused for a little while. I wanted to tell them but it was so ridiculous. I mean, being terrorised by an animal that didn't even exist. I wasn't sure how they'd take it. They might think I'd gone loopy. I took a breath, looking round at my friends. I knew that friendship, love and kindness were everything and yet I couldn't tell them.

"It's nothing…honestly. I'm fine. If you're going to the shops, could you get me a packet of halva please – the Greek one."

"Oooh…and some flapjacks for me, please," added Letty.

The group left, leaving only Letty behind with me.

"Okay," whispered Letty. "Spill!"

"What?"

"Spill the beans before Wilberforce gets here."

"Oh, Letty, I can't. It's so stupid."

"I don't care. Just spill!"

"Promise you won't tell anyone."

"Promise." She smiled, taking the tissue from my nose to check on what it looked like. She released a grimace.

"The last couple of times I've tried to reach my totem, I can't…or if I do, then it leaves me. I end up on my own, under attack from another totem."

"What do you mean?"

"This other totem is trying to kill me."

"I wonder who it belongs to," said Letty, rubbing her chin, probably going through everyone we knew and the totem they were attached to. That's what I'd done – several times.

"What's the animal?" she asked.

I didn't reply.

"Ellery?"

"I can't tell you."

"What's the animal?" she repeated.

"It's a…dragon," I said in a whisper.

"Mother Earth, Ellery! A dragon totem is one of the most powerful totems…maybe the *most* powerful totem."

"You mean, you believe me?"

"Of course I believe you. Why wouldn't I?"

"Because dragons don't exist, do they?"

"They don't exist in the real world. Just because you can't see it in the physical world, it doesn't mean it doesn't exist."

I felt suddenly calm, relieved at my friend's response, although that was soon cancelled out by the thought of the dragon being real.

"Thank you, Miss Keel. That will be all. You may go," ordered Dr Wilberforce, who'd entered the room unnoticed. Letty appeared disappointed that Mitchell hadn't come back with him.

"Apparently there are some great totem books in the Quinton library," said Letty as she opened the heavy old door to leave. "We should check them out," she said with raised eyebrows.

"It looks like it's stopped, dear," said Dr Wilberforce with a disappointed sigh. Perhaps he was hoping to amputate!

***

Our class walked through the countryside to the station and travelled by train to Quinton House in Hampstead. At least there were no slaughterhouses on the agenda this time. Quinton was just as grand as I'd remembered, the large Georgian property screaming historical elegance and beauty. We followed a grumpy Myerscough into the library. I think he'd reverted back to his moodiness from being away from Mum, who remained the librarian for what was left of the Saint Timothy's pupils.

"Welcome, Year 9s," said Mrs Huckabee, who now worked permanently at Quinton House as head of the

Magaecian Circle. "The same rules apply for library books here as last year. Please find something you like, bleep it out and…enjoy!" She looked down at a list in her hand. "Totem and shapeshifting questions with Mrs Laura Mitchell will begin momentarily. This is not compulsory but simply for those with questions from your holiday reading or problems concerning totem changes."

I heaved a sigh of relief. I didn't want to discuss my dragon totem with anyone. At least not yet anyway.

"May I have a show of hands, please, for those needing Mrs Mitchell."

Only three hands went up: Delia Wu, Aldwyn Garrick and Orford – whose hair had now mysteriously returned back to its sleek self. His mum must have sorted it this morning. Mrs Huckabee looked across at me with eyebrows raised as if I'd be wanting a sitting with Mrs Mitchell too. I smiled awkwardly back at her, pretending I had no problems with my totem, resulting in a smile and nod in response.

I sat at a table with Nyle, Kemp, Letty and Thomas. Letty had already taken a totem book and passed me the page on dragon totems.

"A dragon is the symbol of ancient and instinctive power," said Nyle.

"What?" I hissed.

Nyle, Thomas and Kemp immediately stared at Letty.

"They needed to know. We have to work this out together, Ellery," said Letty, slightly red in the face.

I nodded, but I was a little put out after she'd promised not to tell anyone.

I looked at the pages in front of me. The dragon was a master of the elements: earth, air, water and fire.

"You're a lucky cow," said Kemp. "You've got the best ever totem. It's totally Hawk. I'd swap my mouse any day for that one."

"But it's not my totem. Don't you see? It visits me and tries to kill me but it's not mine. It has to belong to someone else."

"Who do you think it could be?" asked Letty, taking back the book.

"Who's going to Mrs Mitchell about totem changes?" said Nyle. "It might be one of them. We know everyone else's totems. No one has a dragon."

"They say a spirit dragon can represent the Devil," added Kemp, appearing more and more pale with every word. "Perhaps it's a warning."

"You should tell Mitchell," said Letty. "*Mr* Mitchell – not Mrs. I can come with you."

"No, not Mitchell," I replied.

"You don't still think he's trying to kill you, do you?" added Letty.

"What? Who told you about that?"

"A small Year 8 girl. She was looking for you this morning. She told me you'd been to her house and that you thought Mitchell was trying to kill you."

"Mika Mitchell," I growled. "No…I think I should go and see Dave…only I'm not sure how I can slip away without being noticed. Myerscough is watching me morning, noon and night."

"Dave's only one or two stops from here," said Letty. "We'll cover for you. Just don't stay at Dave's too long, then

35

you should make it back in good time and no one will be any the wiser, with any luck."

As Nyle got up to find a book, I couldn't help thinking that getting out unnoticed might not be as easy as it sounded. Being the only ebonoid in the school made me a noticeable subject: celebrity status but without the perks. I'd have to wait until later, when it was dark.

"Here we are," said Nyle, slamming a large old and musty book onto the table. Letty spluttered and waved the dust away from her face.

"What's this?" I asked.

"*The Secret Passageways of Quinton House*," answered Nyle. "An old book by Aidan Seeke. Look." He passed across the book. It was all about Quinton House's history. The unusual locks and the secret passageways used years ago in troubled times of war.

"How did you know about this?" I asked. It seemed a very weird book for Nyle to pick up. He was more into sports or magupe.

"We've got a copy at home. My dad's a locksmith, remember? He loves this kind of stuff. He told me to read it before coming to Quinton House last year."

"And did you?" asked Letty.

He pulled a funny face which was an obvious *no*.

I took the book and examined the moth-eaten cover.

"Dad said there's a tunnel or passage that runs under Quinton House that was used during the war when London was being bombed. It's on our history curriculum for next term."

"What's that about the curriculum?" asked Delia, who'd

obviously overheard us and rushed over to investigate. "How do you know what's on the curriculum next term?"

"My dad told me. He said it was what triggered his interest in doors and locks and stuff. He said it was the best lesson he ever had at Quinton when he was a boy. Really good fun. Apparently, one of the teachers takes you through the passage."

"Where does it go?" I asked.

"Outside, of course," answered Nyle, which wasn't nearly enough information to ease my worried thoughts.

"We'll come with you," said Thomas, rubbing his hands together.

"No," I replied. "Myerscough will be onto us."

"But he's your dad," said Letty. "He's bound to let you get away with stuff."

"I wish," I said, rolling my eyes. "He thinks I might *zap* someone with negativity. Besides, he'll notice if there's a whole load of empty beds. Let me do this by myself. If I'm not back by morning, then you can report me missing, okay?"

Nyle took back the book and started flicking through the pages.

Delia went looking for another copy on the shelves.

3

THE GREAT ESCAPE

I lay in bed, under the covers, fully clothed until I was sure everyone in the room was asleep. It felt like hours had passed as I watched the shadows creep slowly across the ceiling. An old church bell chimed eleven times in the distance. I glanced at my watch, then glanced again. I made my decision to go. I only hoped I could get to Dave and back without being missed. Timing was essential and the seconds were already ticking. I crept from the room, closing the door carefully behind me. The lack of modern lighting through the corridors brought a funny sensation to my insides as I headed for the kitchen. Shadows hid behind every wall. I didn't believe in ghosts but I half expected one to jump out and get me at any moment. Another flickering shadow caught my attention from a gloomy corner. I glanced over briefly. Nothing there. An uneasy feeling ran through me. I couldn't shake it off – a worrying sense that I wasn't alone.

"Pssst!"

My heart left my chest to exit through my mouth. "What are you doing here, Nyle?" I blurted out, then lowered my voice to a whisper, shaking at the noise I'd just made. "I was meant to be doing this by myself."

"I know...but surely your parents have warned you never to go out in the dark unaccompanied," he said with a smirk.

"What?"

"Come on. There's no time to argue. I'm coming with you, and that's that."

"But—"

"Here," he said, kneeling down to crawl under the old kitchen work table.

"What are you doing?"

"It's here – ouch!" he answered, banging his head on the underside of the table.

I so wanted to shush him but someone might have heard. I crawled underneath to join him as he pointed out a small metal ring poking out of the floor tile.

"It's a trapdoor," he whispered as he yanked it up.

My stomach became a bag of worms, wriggling out of control as I peered through the opening to a set of stone stairs twisting steeply into blackness.

"What's down there?" I asked.

"It's the secret passage to the outside, of course. You don't want to get caught, do you?"

"The secret passage?"

"Yes."

"How can you be so sure?"

"What else could it be? My dad said he went down it so it's got to be okay."

"Really? But that's when he was at school. I mean, how old's your dad? That must've been a long time ago, Nyle."

"It'll be fine."

"Do you know *exactly* where it goes?"

"Kind of."

"Kind of?"

"It must lead outside somewhere."

"That's not very reassuring. We could end up anywhere."

"It doesn't matter, Ellery. So long as we get out of Quinton House without being seen, right?"

"I suppose," I said, looking down the stairwell into an abyss of uncertainty. I felt those worms again and chewed on a fingernail. "Are you sure this is okay?"

"Of course. Anyway, I brought this," he said, taking out a torch from his rucksack. "It was a birthday present from my parents." He waved it about in front of my face.

We followed the stairs deep underground, lit only by the narrow yellow beam of light from Nyle's torch. The walls glistened along the damp, unfriendly passage. The smell of mildew coupled with the rhythmic dripping of water was enough to unsettle my stomach from writhing worms into a stabbing spasm. I tried to balance myself, feeling the wall beside me, slimy and unpleasant. My breath quickened. *Pat-pat-pat* echoed round the walls as we ventured further. We must've disturbed an army of rats. My thoughts flashed back to Kemp's mouse totem. That little mouse saved my life last year. Rats were similar to mice – just bigger – *with beady eyes that freaked people out.* I decided to stop thinking.

We walked for ages through the slippery passageway, clammy and cold with barely enough headroom to stand.

"You do know we need to be back in time for breakfast tomorrow, don't you?"

"Light!" cried Nyle, pointing ahead. As we moved further through the tunnel towards the light it opened out into a large cavern. A couple of vertical rays of moonlight punctured through a circle at the top.

"Is that a manhole cover?" asked Nyle.

From where I was standing, it looked no bigger than a bath plug. My throat felt suddenly dry. It was obvious that the only way out was up. A very long and narrow iron ladder hung sadly from the wall beneath it. Its metal restraints corroded away into an orange, pointy mesh, sending weird, misshapen shadows to stretch out towards us.

"That doesn't look very safe," I said. "What now?"

"It'll be fine," said Nyle, removing his rucksack. He took out a book and shone the torch on a page with a diagram. "This looks about right."

"Nyle Pinkerton, please tell me that isn't the book from the Quinton House library."

"What do you mean?" he retorted.

"I mean, a book with a tracking device is not really what we want down here."

"Oops! It's okay. We'll be back before anyone notices. Stop stressing over nothing and just follow me." He put the book and the torch back in his bag which meant that we'd have to climb the unsteady ladder in a disconcerting inky darkness. I followed behind Nyle, a sudden chill running through me as if someone had dropped a tray of ice cubes down my back. Every instinct screamed *stop!* as I squeezed my fingers around the rungs of the ladder. With no other choice but to continue, each clambering step was accompanied by an unnerving creak. With each creak came a treacherous sway. With each sway, panic bubbled up my throat. Onwards and upwards, shuddering and pausing. I got into a kind of automatic rhythm behind Nyle and calmed myself slightly until I did the one thing no one should ever do on a ladder…I looked down. A storm of adrenaline invaded my arms and legs, rendering them useless and wobbly. A hindrance I could've done without as I hugged the ladder, making it even more unsteady with my shaking body. I squeezed it. Couldn't let go. Couldn't go up. Couldn't go down.

"What's happening?" Nyle called down to me, obviously realising I'd stopped following him.

I said nothing, too afraid to even move my mouth.

"It's too late to turn back now. Come on, Ellery. We're almost there. You can do it. You know you can. Listen to my spell."

I'd got used to the Magaecian term "spell", which was just another name for a group of words and sentences made up of *spellings*. Although I understood only too well about the power of words and of the effect they might have on a person, I couldn't help wishing instead that they were *magic* spells and not just normal words of encouragement, as a cascade of salty tears dropped over my lips.

"Look at me, Ellery."

I took a deep breath and looked up at Nyle while still clinging hard to the ladder like a long-lost friend.

"One step at a time, Ellery. Keep looking up. Focus only on me. So close. A couple more steps. Just a few. Five steps more. Three steps more. One step more." He grabbed my wrist. "Look."

I'd reached the top. Who'd have thought I'd find a manhole cover to be the most wonderful thing I'd ever seen? Nyle pushed and punched at it, trying to force it open but it was so heavy. He removed his rucksack which was throwing him off balance and chucked it to the ground. I didn't follow its long descent – I'd have thrown up and fallen for sure.

Nyle pushed with more force.

"Push harder," I shouted, releasing an echoing, *push harder, harder, harder*. Perched behind Nyle, I tried to reach the cover too, keeping one hand firmly on the ladder but it was too far to stretch with unreliable jelly-legs.

"Hold my ankles," said Nyle. "I'm going to give it my biggest push with a bit more *oomph* but I don't want to lose my footing."

I held his ankles while he tried his *oomphiest* push. A sharp crack of light appeared as the cover budged. He carried on, scraping the heavy cover further and further across the outer surface until moonlight flooded in. This should have been a relief, a moment to celebrate but it wasn't. I felt giddy and lost my balance. The ladder protested with a sudden, untimely convulsion. It released itself from the insecure holdings, leaving me clinging to Nyle's ankles as it juddered down the wall. The sound of metal clanging against stone echoed through the tunnel. I dangled back and forth like a faulty pendulum as the ladder finally crashed to the floor, throwing up a very large cloud of smoke, filled with mould, dirt and possibly rodents. The whole tunnel shook with a grumble. Nyle, now screaming like a girl, tried his best to pull himself up through the manhole to civilisation, but he wasn't strong enough with me attached, swinging like a dead weight from his feet.

"You're too heavy," he gasped.

"Don't let go, Nyle," I cried. I squeezed my eyes so tightly shut, my eyeballs almost retracted into the back of my head. Perhaps I should have let go, saved my friend, but I couldn't. If I fell from here, I doubt I'd live to tell the tale. I needed to focus. I needed to calm down. Negative thoughts could only turn into ebonoid energy, which would hurt Nyle. Then we'd both fall. I kept my eyes shut and tried to think of something positive – anything. The first thing that came into my head was the smell of my mum's freshly baked bread and Lionel's wagging tail, always waiting for fallen crumbs. It didn't work. In fact, it made things worse as a cold sweat accompanied my sense of dread.

A sudden gust of icy air blew through the tunnel. I felt its force as it surged through my lungs, whirling at such a rate I should have struggled to breathe but I didn't. Instead, it seemed to enhance all my senses as if a power had awoken within me. My tongue felt strangely tingly. Nyle's knuckles turned white as he did everything in his power to hang on.

"It's no good. I'm losing my grip, Ellery," he screamed.

"Hang on, Nyle. You can do it."

He couldn't do it. He let go…

We should have plummeted to our end. We should have. To say luck was on our side that night is probably a massive understatement. It was nothing short of a miracle as another icy gust rushed through the tunnel, whipping us up in a swirling tornado of grime and sludge, hurling us high through the air before spitting us out hard onto the ground outside like unwanted chewing gum. Dazed, choking and spluttering, I coughed up the unavoidable stray bits of leaves and dirt. Nyle looked like he was about to throw up into a nearby bush.

"What the…" spluttered Nyle, wiping his mouth on his sleeve. "I mean, how the…" He paused again to catch his breath. "What actually happened in there?"

I didn't know for sure. All I did know was that we were somehow still in one piece.

"It's called luck, Nyle."

As chance would have it, the manhole came up right next to Hampstead Heath. I knelt down to catch my breath, wondering just how we really had managed to make it without killing ourselves.

"Come on." I shuddered with an afterthought of what could have happened. "Hampstead Heath station's just a couple of minutes from here, I'm sure of it. We can get a train to West Hampstead, then change to go on to Wembley Park."

"Do you think there's a match on tonight?" asked Nyle.

"You're not serious?"

"Just kidding. It would be over by now anyway."

We continued on to Dave's along the busy main road, which was clogged with traffic even at this time of night. We both remembered the way. It was such a relief to see her front door as Nyle rang the bell with a shaky hand.

"Children. What are you doing here? It's so late," said Dave softly, so softly in fact that it was almost a whisper.

45

This was not the greeting I'd expected. Dave, always so calm and reassuring, seemed different tonight, jumpy and on edge, scanning the street as we walked inside.

"Come into the kitchen," she said.

A delicious aroma of hot chocolate wafted over from her stove and two mugs stood ready on the sideboard. I wondered how she knew we'd be coming.

"Do your teachers know you're here?" she asked.

We both looked down at her kitchen table, then back at her.

"You must stop wandering off, children. It's not safe."

"Why?" I asked. "Is Nash back?"

"Nash is the least of your worries," she replied. "There are many bad people on the streets these days, especially Dwellers with no money. You would be a soft target."

"Sorry," I said. "It's just – I really need your help, Dave. Please help me. Please."

"My child, you're distressed. What is it?"

"It's my totem, it won't stay with me. It leaves me so that I'm vulnerable, under attack. There's a…" I stopped before inserting the word *dragon*. "There's another totem that keeps appearing and it's trying to kill me."

"I see. Do you know who this totem belongs to?" asked Dave.

I shook my head.

"Have you seen this animal anywhere else? During your summer break, perhaps – in the park, at the cinema?"

"It's not actually a *real* animal, Dave."

Dave's face lost its smile. "A dragon?" she asked.

"Yes, it is."

46

"Is it Nash?" asked Nyle.

"No," said Dave. "It's not Nash but it is exactly what Nash saw when he was your age."

"What does it mean, Dave?" I asked.

Dave was about to answer when the doorbell rang, followed by a loud knock.

"You must go, children. It's not safe for you here."

"Why not?" blasted Nyle, sounding a bit rude.

Dave put her finger to her lips to shush him. "Listen to me, children. You must leave through the back." She stopped for a minute, then shouted towards the door, "I'm just coming!"

"Okay. Take your time," answered a woman's voice through the letterbox.

Somewhere, buried deep in my memory, I had a feeling I should've known who that voice belonged to.

"Who is that, Dave?" I asked.

"You *must* go. Listen to me, Ellery. Don't do what Nash did. You need that dragon on your side. Now go, *please*."

We did as we were told and left through the French doors into her back garden, over the fence and onto the street to walk back to the station.

"What was that all about?" asked Nyle. "We didn't even get a hot chocolate."

"I know. She was expecting someone. Did you recognise that woman's voice?"

Nyle shrugged, shaking his head. "I wonder what she meant about not doing what Nash did," he said.

I didn't reply, my head spinning with unanswered questions.

"Oh no!" cried Nyle, covering his mouth.

"What's wrong?"

"How are we going to get back into school without being caught? We can't go back the way we came…unless you've got a couple of fold-up parachutes in your pocket."

"It was a long way down, wasn't it?" I added, biting my lip. "Aren't there any other secret passageways into Quinton? What does it say in that book of yours?"

Nyle felt for his rucksack. "Noooooo!"

"We've left the book in the passage, haven't we?" I said, through gritted teeth. "We'll have to go back for it."

"I'm not free-falling through that manhole, Ellery. Forget it. We'll have to go in through the pig flap in the kitchen door at the back of Quinton."

"Pig flap?"

"It's a big dog flap, really. It was put in for Kessie last year."

I giggled at the thought of a pig squashing through a dog flap. This was replaced with a wave of anger. "Why didn't we go through the pig flap in the first place, instead of that bloody death-trap tunnel?"

"I didn't know it was going to be broken. Besides, we'd probably have got caught going through the flap anyway."

The sudden scarlet blush on Nyle's face couldn't mask the obvious fact that he hadn't thought about using the flap to leave Quinton House. Also, if we might have got caught leaving through it, there'd be a strong possibility we'd get caught arriving through it.

"I suppose, once we're in the kitchen, we can go back down through the trap door and retrieve the book," added Nyle.

"In the pitch-black?"

"Mother Earth! It was a straight path. We'll manage."

We caught the train to Hampstead, which was almost empty, then trudged up the hill to Quinton House. Darkness reigned through the grounds, throwing menacing shadows over the stately building. Silhouettes of tree branches swayed like withered fingers to point us out and give us away. We made for the back entrance as quickly and quietly as we could, praying we wouldn't be seen. Clinging to the wall, we edged our way to the back kitchen door, hesitating with every rustle of leaves or windy whoosh. Nyle was right about the flap. It was there all right. He crouched down and peeked through it, then turned to me with a thumbs up.

I'll go first, he silent-spelled me. My friends and I were quite good at silent spells, which were more or less the same as using sign language. As Nyle used both hands to do this he accidentally let the flap swing back with a clap.

Panic flooded through me. It took all my effort to hold still as I was shaking so much. We both paused for a moment. No lights flashed on. No door flew open…but they still could at any moment. Nyle let out a puff then turned and slid through the flap head first. He took ages as his shoulders, which had become quite broad over the summer, struggled through the tight space. Once his feet had disappeared, I unclenched my teeth and took a breath. I lowered myself level with the flap, squeezing my eyes closed as I ventured in. I felt like a penguin as I clambered through, wondering if I'd get wedged between the inside and the outside. Blood pounded through my head as I emerged through the flap and into the kitchen. A sixth sense sent prickles down my spine. That's when I lost the ability to move as shaking took over and I got pins and needles in my arms. I could hear the sound of my own breathing, a deafening sound as I focused on a large shiny pair of lace-up shoes in front of my nose. They didn't belong to Nyle.

"Let me help you," said Mr Butterly, his voice stern and cold.

My insides tightened so violently I could scarcely breathe. I wanted to close up like a telescope and vanish backwards through the flap but instead, Butterly dragged me up to my feet, his stony face reprimanding me more than any words.

"I-I can explain, sir," I pleaded.

4

HEAVE-HO!

"Sit down, please," demanded Butterly, pulling over two chairs with a loud scrape – one for me and one for Nyle. He then began making a hot chocolate. I really needed one and I could see Nyle licking his lips from the corner of my eye.

Myerscough emerged from under the kitchen work table, carrying Nyle's green rucksack.

"Yours?" he said, throwing it at Nyle before sending a grunt my way.

Mr Butterly poured out two steaming mugs of hot chocolate. One he handed to Myerscough, the other he kept for himself. Nyle's shoulders dropped and I suspect mine did too.

"Right," began Butterly, after a slurp. "Who wants to start?"

Nyle stood up. His face, splattered with dark brown

smudges of dirt, his hair damp and matted. His eyes darted nervously from side to side.

"Sleepwalking!" announced Nyle, glancing at me. The word had fallen from his mouth in a muddle, lingering in the air like a bad smell.

The bag of worms returned to my stomach; I knew full well that his concocted tale would most likely get us into more trouble. I interrupted before he'd have time to come up with any more rubbish.

"Please, Mr Buttery – *Butterly*." Nyle's eyes almost popped out of his head. I was so nervous Peter Butterly's name turned for a split second into Thomas's idea of *peanut buttery*. I took a breath before starting again.

"It was entirely my fault, sir."

Nyle protested but I didn't let him get a word in.

"I'm sorry, sir," I continued. "It really was nothing to do with Nyle. I've been feeling out of my depth, unable to control my *gift*. I needed to be away from here, away from my friends and the people I care about. I didn't want to risk hurting them, sir, so I left. Nyle followed me to try to stop me."

"I see," replied Butterly, his face like stone. "I appreciate your honesty and also your concern for the safety of your friends, but by leaving without permission, quite a novel exit through the Quinton tunnel, I might add, you managed to put everyone here in danger – not to mention yourselves. That tunnel has been closed to students for over a decade now, due to safety issues."

"What a surprise," muttered Nyle sarcastically, under his breath.

I rolled my eyes at him.

"You see, as teachers, it's our responsibility to make sure all pupils remain secure in our care. If you insist on disappearing, then we, as teachers, must at least *try* to find you. This means that those who search for you may put themselves into a risky situation, and it also means that we're left with fewer staff here to look after the students still remaining."

I said nothing, looking down at my dirty trainers.

"We have rules for a reason, Ellery. If you choose not to follow them, then perhaps this type of institution is not suited to your needs and perhaps you should consider an alternative form of education."

Was he expelling me? My throat grew tight and achy. I didn't want to leave. I put my hands together in namaste. I knew I couldn't allow myself to become angry.

"Please give me another chance, sir. Please."

"You've got to learn to listen, Ellery. You can still have an open mind but the act of listening is vital if you're to avoid repeatedly making poor decisions. Value the importance of honesty. The truth will always be more powerful than the untruth."

My face felt hot. He saw straight through me.

"Let me tell you something. When I was at school, many years ago, my best friend was a boy called Simeon Nash."

My eyes widened. I wasn't exactly sure where he was going with this.

"Yes, later known as Saxon Nash, of course. He was a very likeable character: funny, intelligent, kind and a most loyal friend. Nothing like the character you encountered last year. Not so very unlike how you are now, in fact. He chose not to seek help and not to listen to those able to advise him. Please be careful not to do the same. We can help you here but you've got to want to be helped. Stop distrusting those who care for you." He looked across to Myerscough. "Distrust is a negative energy. It narrows your world considerably."

"Yes, sir," I said, glancing at Myerscough.

"Now go to bed, both of you."

"Yes, sir. Thank you, sir," I said, which Nyle repeated.

"In the meantime, you will both receive a yellow on your rainbow – *only* a yellow, I might add, because I expect you to find a way to make it up to me during the term. Now if you'll excuse me." He bowed his head with a nod, picked up his hot chocolate and left the kitchen.

Nyle let out a huge puff of relief. We were lucky not to be expelled.

"Ellery," barked Myerscough. "A word, please." He looked across to Nyle, still standing there. *"Alone."*

My heart sank. I wasn't feeling up to another lecture and certainly not from Myerscough. I silent-spelled a *sorry* to Nyle who signed a *good luck* back to me which Myerscough saw.

"Ellery," he began.

"Yes, sir."

"Don't call me that," he snapped.

"What?"

"I'm your teacher during school times but I'm first and foremost your father."

That's not the way I saw it.

"Look – I know I'm not doing a very good job of it but being a father is a new position for me. I'm trying my best but it's pretty obvious that I'm making a pig's ear of it. Do you have any idea how I felt when you thought I was plotting to kill you? Kill my own daughter! What kind of a monster do you think I am?"

"I'm sorry, sir – I mean, I'm sorry…" I couldn't say the word *Dad*.

"No. I'm the one that should be sorry. I've lost you once, I can't lose you again, Ellery. I will always be on your side. You *must* understand that. Always."

I nodded, unable to answer, a terrible guilt holding me silent. He was right. How could I have thought such a dreadful thing of someone whose only crime was to leave me and Mum in order to keep us safe – tortured to protect us?

"Every time you take off without telling me, my whole body aches. How can I prove to you that I love you, Ellery? What do you want me to do? I know you can't feel the same way about me and I don't blame you for that—"

"No…it's not that. I didn't mean to hurt you," I interrupted, my throat tight again and my eyes prickling as a couple of tears escaped.

"I'm trying my best but you're going to have to be patient."

"I know," I answered, wiping the tears from my cheeks. "I'm sorry…really, I am," I continued, almost swallowing the words as I gulped.

"Come 'ere." He smiled, pulling me hard into his chest. I tried to put my arms around him but he was too wide.

"Whether you like it or not, you're my flesh and blood and I'm going to make sure you don't get into harm's way… but you've got to listen to me."

I nodded again.

"Here," he said, passing me the rest of his hot chocolate. "Finish it off, then you should get some sleep. Big day tomorrow."

Myerscough kissed me on the forehead, then left me alone in the dimly lit kitchen. Eerie shadows clung to the walls, making me gulp down the remains of the hot drink, to get out of the spooky room as quickly as possible. My chest filled with an uncomfortable heat, like I'd swallowed a burning coal. I hurried back to the girls' dormitory with a sense of foreboding at the thought of going to sleep. However, for the first time in weeks, I felt so exhausted, I was out for the count as soon as my head hit the pillow. A deep, deep sleep, void of any dragons.

It should have been just what I needed if it weren't for the *squeak*. I snapped myself awake. I heard it again, moving across the room. Closer and closer, the squeaky sound on the polished floor. I saw no one but it was dark and my eyes needed to adjust. Then…I felt it. A cold sensation tickling at my hand which I retracted as if I'd been burned. My insides curdled as I made out its outline – some sort of snake? I wanted to put the light on but that would have woken everybody, and I was already in enough trouble as it was. I tried to stretch out nearer to the moonlight, which was making its way into the room through the threadbare dormitory curtains. It wasn't a snake. It was a worm, I think. Too small for a snake and yet, far too big for an earthworm. As I gawped at it, it returned the stare, observing me with virtually no eyes, and a strangely melancholy expression. Perhaps it was a mythical creature like the dragon. It wasn't segmented or slimy like a worm but scalier with a couple of small spiky bits on its head and neck. I couldn't recall any myths about over-sized scaly worms, so maybe not. I put out my hand as a non-threatening gesture, encouraging it to come nearer. It seemed pleased and slid towards me onto my hand, almost reaching my elbow, full length. I wanted to wake Letty but didn't want to make any sudden moves in case I dropped it. I brought it closer to my face, my pulse racing as my heart thumped against my ribs.

It puffed at me.

"Eeew!" The smell of this creature's breath was unbelievably offensive as if it must have slid along the Quinton House sewage pipes and then mixed in with some gone-off fish. I pinched my nose with my fingers in disgust, accidentally dropping the worm on the floor. It rolled into a ball, then slithered out of the room. I didn't see where it went, too busy covering my face with my pillow, trying my best to inhale the smell of fresh linen instead of the obnoxious lingering fish-poo-odour. Gagging, I tried to remove myself from the extremely unpleasant smell but it was stuck in my nose and wouldn't budge. My stomach squeezed violently. My throat clenched but the hot feeling rising upwards could not be stopped as I heaved involuntarily to release the contents of my dinner – tomatoey smoky bean casserole mixed in with the sludge brown of my partially digested hot chocolate to create a masterpiece of puke-art.

"Gross!" screamed Delia Wu, leaping from the bed next to mine, almost splashing into my vomit.

"I'll get help," Letty said, heaving, and covering her nose, obviously happy to leave the room as quickly as possible.

One by one, each girl awoke, every scream of disgust and horror louder than the last. Mass hysteria forced them to race to the door to escape the carnage, some gagging in the process. Poor Angela Yin threw up as well, sending Paige Livingstone flying through the resultant slippery goo. It was a stench disaster. An apocalyptic barf bonanza.

"Follow me, dear," said Dr Ramsay. She must've heard the commotion down the corridor and come to investigate. I reckon our screams were heard as far as the next county.

Dazed and disorientated, I followed my teacher, unaware of what was ensuing around me. Myerscough found me and helped me once I'd washed off. He didn't ask any questions, just took me to his room which had a large green sofa in it – most likely the same colour as my new complexion.

"You take the bed. I'll take the sofa," he said.

I didn't argue, feeling only too grateful for a room that was heave-free. He sat with me until I settled. I wasn't sure if I'd dreamt about seeing the strange worm or if it really had visited me. I couldn't smell its dreadful stench any more and now that I was away from the room of retch and regurgitation, I calmed down and fell back to sleep.

***

Morning came too soon. My eyes felt heavy as I looked around – Myerscough was gone. Shrill screams from outside the room forced me to get up and see what was going on. Perhaps someone else had come across the worm. I peeked round the door but it was Kessie in the corridor, eating someone's socks.

"Hurry up!" shouted Mr Ademola, coaxing Kessie away from the stairs and towards the kitchen. The large pig refused to let go of the socks until Ademola offered her some sort of dog biscuit.

I went back to my dorm to get washed and dressed. It smelled strongly of disinfectant. Traipsing into the dining hall, my mood lifted immediately. Smoothies and shakes, donk, tofu scramble, smoky tempeh, porridge, pancakes and a selection of brightly coloured fruits. I hadn't lost my appetite.

"You okay?" asked Letty, tapping a place for me next to her.

"Is it true you puked all over everyone last night?" shouted Aldwyn Garrick at the top of his voice.

"Yeh," replied Nyle. "It's cos we sneaked out to the pub and got hammered. Ellery drank sixteen pints."

Nyle's quick response totally silenced Aldwyn. I tried my best to look serious as he glanced across the table at me, then back at Nyle, who raised his eyebrows. Aldwyn picked up some donk, then scurried off without a word.

"Nice one, Nyle," I said with a giggle.

"What happened at Dave's?" asked Letty.

"Is it true you got caught and called the head Mr *Buttery*?" asked Kemp.

"You never did," gasped Letty.

I nodded. "Nyle and I got a yellow."

"You're lucky your dad's a teacher here – if that had been someone else, they'd have been expelled for sure," said Kemp.

"It was worth it to get help from Dave," said Letty.

"Actually, it wasn't," snapped Nyle. "Her advice was about as useful as a chocolate teapot."

"Did you say she had a chocolate teapot?" asked Thomas.

"Why didn't she help you?" said Letty, ignoring Thomas's question.

"She was expecting someone – someone she didn't want us to see," I added.

"Who?" asked Thomas.

"I don't know," I replied. "When I asked her, she wouldn't tell me."

"What did she say about the dragon?" asked Kemp, spreading peanut butter on a slice of donk.

"She said I needed it on my side and that I shouldn't do what Nash did."

"What's that meant to mean?" asked Thomas, his chocolate moustache making it difficult to take him seriously.

"Apparently, Nash saw the same dragon when he was my age," I began. "What do you think Nash did that I shouldn't do?"

"He must have tried to kill it," said Kemp.

"Maybe the dragon was Darwin Burgess's totem and that's why he tried to kill it," said Thomas.

"But Burgess is dead," I replied. "It can't belong to him."

"Maybe the dragon represents all Dwellers, so by killing the dragon, Nash would kill off the Dwellers?" added Kemp, narrowing his eyes like a young detective.

"Eat up," said Mitchell, poking his head between me and Letty. Letty's face went so red it looked as though she'd got a sudden case of sunburn. "We've a long hike today."

"Where are we going, sir?" I asked.

"We're beginning our journey with a lesson of practical spells, then heading on to a city farm."

"Is it far away, sir?" asked Thomas, reaching for his hot chocolate as if a swig would somehow calm him down if it were.

"Two and a half hours tops. Don't worry. You have legs. You'll be fine. Year 12 will be meeting us there."

Thomas's face lost its colour.

"I'm sure it'll be fine. Don't worry, Thomas," I said quietly.

"Finish up, please!" yelled Myerscough – although he wasn't really yelling, his voice was just naturally shouty. "Clear away, then get jackets, rucksacks and hiking boots, and meet by the main entrance of Quinton House where Mr Butterly will address you. You have fifteen minutes – no more."

We followed his instructions, gathering our belongings to reach the entrance with a couple of minutes to spare. A group of teachers mumbled in a corner, looking round every so often with anxious faces. Something deep inside, an instinct perhaps, gave me a funny feeling. I knew if I questioned Myerscough about it, he'd probably make up some flaky story to keep me from feeling scared, which ultimately, was far scarier.

Mr Butterly approached, holding his hand up to capture our attention and silence us as he spoke.

"This is a very exciting moment," he began. "The start of your term's peregrination. Years 9 and 12 are the only years to have no statutory exams. Year 10, of course, is the travel year, and these pupils have already set off for their long journey across foreign lands." He looked at each and every one of us.

"Listen to your teachers, strengthen your community and camaraderie and reprogramme your minds for the better. Attempt to make a difference. Be an optimist. Optimism is an empowering force. Focus on what can still be done to stop Magae from getting rid of us and not on what has been done already to endanger us." Butterly looked directly at me when he said this. "We shouldn't see Dwellers as our enemy, they are but ignorant and ill-informed. Find a way to teach them to acknowledge what is enough. Set an example, and by human nature they will follow." He paused then added, "Have a great term." He smiled and bowed in a gesture of namaste which we all mimicked.

Mr Ademola led the class towards the ornate gates where Myerscough stood sternly, gesturing for me to leave the line.

"I think you should sit this one out after last night."

"But I'm fine," I replied, stamping my foot. I just drank the hot chocolate too quickly – that's all. I want to go... please."

"No. If it's a bug, then you'll pass it round."

"Well, it's a bit late now. I've just had breakfast with everyone, haven't I?"

"Mind that tone, Ellery," said Myerscough, pointing his finger at me.

"I was with Ellery all evening," said Nyle, edging his way into our conversation, his face looking a bit red. "I would have it too by now, if it were a bug."

"I'm willing to chance it," Letty chirped.

"Me too," added Thomas, echoed by most of the class bar one or two like Aldwyn Garrick and Teddy Wade until they saw Orford Nibley-Soames volunteer to chance it as well.

Myerscough shook his head in resignation. He glanced back at a small commotion from another cluster of teachers in the garden, talking over one another. I'm sure I overheard Nash's name passed around once or twice, which unnerved me a bit.

"All right," blasted Myerscough turning back to us. "I'll be coming with you."

"Great," I mumbled under my breath. "Maybe I should fetch some nappies and a rattle."

"At least he's letting you come," whispered Letty.

Glancing back briefly at the unease among the teachers, my instinct was warning me that danger might be catching up with us before too long.

5

THE FOUNTAIN OF FURY

"Practical spells," began Myerscough, "are not as straightforward as you might think. Not all spells work on all people. You have to choose your receiver or perhaps cast your spell through someone else in order to get it to work."

I watched my classmates' heads nodding. I wondered how everybody else seemed to understand what he was on about while I had absolutely no idea. As we walked past shops and expensive boutiques, Letty pointed out a pair of red shoes that looked just like a pair her aunt had bought online. Myerscough and Mitchell stopped at a small bench, just opposite a crowd of young activists. University students, perhaps. They were protesting outside the entrance of a local butcher. Holding flyers of tortured animals, their faces were reddened, their eyes narrowed and menacing. Some carried buckets full of blood – probably not real blood but it looked realistic enough.

"What do you think about this?" asked Mitchell, swaying his head in the direction of the activists on the other side of the road. He nodded at Vikesh who had his hand raised.

"I don't blame them," said Vikesh. "They're right. No one should mistreat animals in that way."

"How many passers-by are stopping to engage with them?" continued Mitchell.

"No one's stopping," answered Thomas.

"Exactly," agreed Mitchell. "Why do you think that is?"

"They're being too aggressive," said Letty. "Those pictures are horrific. I don't think anyone really wants to be confronted by that…not ever."

"But people need to know these things go on," said Vikesh.

"Yes, they do need to know these things go on," agreed Mitchell, "but this is a local butcher, not a supermarket chain. This Dweller man or woman will be a hard-working individual, trying to earn an honest living in a difficult world. They might get their meat from a small organic holding that practises a more humane style of slaughter."

"There's no such thing," whispered Letty with a shudder.

"As Magaecians, we choose not to harm animals in any way. We don't require animal products to stay alive and nourished, but we still need to show an element of empathy to those in the meat trade. How will they live without selling meat? They'd need an alternative occupation. This doesn't happen overnight. This is why activists in this type of scenario so often fail. You can't just expect a butcher to pack up shop when there are bills to pay – not without a backup plan and immediate money-earning opportunities."

"But protesting can change things," said Thomas.

"Yes, Mr Marks, but we need, as activists, to seek out what it is that we want in the long run from our protest. Is it to stop people eating meat? Is it to stop cruelty to animals? Is it to reduce our carbon footprint?"

"It's all of those, isn't it?" I said.

"Sure," replied Mitchell with a smile. "But we won't do it like this. This is bullying. People don't respond well to bullying. No one wants to be preached to or judged. People need to know they've made the decision to alter their habits off their own bat, not by being forced in this way. Sure, they need to know all the information, be educated on why they need to change their habits and the benefits of doing so, of course…but there are better ways. Magaecians are very good at this. We do it by creating the right spell. We know that *little changes can have a big impact*." He paused for a moment. "Wait here."

Mitchell left the group to cross the road to the activists, leaving us with Myerscough.

"What do you think Mr Mitchell is saying?" asked Myerscough.

"Move away and stop bullying people!" shouted Thomas.

"No," said Myerscough, scowling.

"He's teaching them new spells, isn't he?" I said.

"Yes, he is." Myerscough nodded.

The activists collected together to listen to Mitchell. One of them, possibly their leader – well-built and tanned, wearing ripped jeans – shouted and pointed his finger violently, first at the shop, then at Mitchell. He had a large spider's web tattooed on his neck and an emerald streak running through his hair. He obviously wasn't going to change his opinion. In fact, none of them seemed keen at all to stop their protest, apart from, that is, a young girl, tall, blonde and slim with circular glasses. She seemed mesmerised by Mr Mitchell. She stood so still, as if she'd been frozen in time. She approached Mitchell, handing him her flyer, then put her bucket of blood down onto the pavement. Mitchell took her aside, raising his hand to stop jeers from the rest of the group. The girl nodded and smiled as she listened to Mitchell's spells, then, after a while, she shook Mitchell's hand, before going back to regroup with her colleagues.

"I don't understand," began Thomas, watching Mitchell cross back to us. "They've let a woman walk straight into the butcher's to buy meat. Did Mr Mitchell tell them to stop what they were doing and give up?"

"What did you say to them, sir?" I asked Mitchell as he got back to our class.

"But the woman still went into the shop to buy meat," confirmed Thomas, furrowing his brow.

"Yes, she did," said Mitchell. "I tried to explain to the *well-meaning* vegans that we were vegans too but that by casting spells in this way, they were destined to fail. A slightly different approach with a change of spell was all that was necessary."

"But that bloke was wagging his finger at you. He was so cross," said Letty.

"Yeah, he was." Mitchell laughed. "I knew my spell wouldn't work on him but I knew it might work on one of the others."

"The girl with the glasses," I said.

Mitchell raised his eyebrows.

"It was bound to work on her," whispered Letty. "I mean, look at him. Who's going to say no to Mr Mitchell?"

"I wonder if she gave him her phone number as well," Kemp said, sniggering.

"What was that, Mr Barclay?" asked Myerscough.

"Nothing, sir."

"But the customers still bought meat," said Thomas. "I don't understand."

"Rome wasn't built in a day, Mr Marks," replied Mitchell. "We can't expect Dwellers to give up meat in one single day, but we can ask them to cut down on it, or at least buy meat that's been reared humanely. Remember the old *supply and demand*? They demand less, so butchers will supply less…and so it goes on until we're all better off – especially Magae. Find the right spell, and it will work."

"So spells don't work all the time, sir?" I asked.

"Sometimes you just have to find the right person on which they will work."

"So your spell worked on the blonde girl?" I asked.

"Yes, I think it did. It'll be up to her to explain with her own spell – or as Dwellers might say, *in her own words* – how changing the spells of the group, choosing carefully the words she suggests they should use, will in turn, achieve a result in their favour. There is a place for activism, of course, but I'm not sure that this is that place – not today."

"Activists," spat Myerscough. "Always taking a violent stand against something or someone. They need to realise that they shouldn't be against everyone but instead *for* everyone. That includes all life on Magae, not just humans."

68

I nodded. I think I got it.

"Okay – take a drink, then we'll be heading for the farm. It's a bit of a walk still," said Myerscough.

Although I'd recovered from last night's bilious attack, I wasn't quite myself yet. I felt weak and my stomach was sore.

"Drink this," said Myerscough, shoving a water flask into my chest. I tightened my lips as I took the flask and unscrewed it. I had to unclench my teeth to take a swig without dribbling it everywhere. I screwed back the lid and threw it back at him, hitting him on the side of the head by accident.

He turned on me like a wild animal.

"Sorry," I said quickly. "Thanks for the water."

Myerscough's face was neutral, utterly void of any expression as he gave me a sarcastic thumbs up. I pursed my lips to remind my mouth to keep shut and avoid *thanks for treating me like a six-year-old in front of my friends* slipping through the cracks.

The farm didn't seem as far away as our teachers wanted us to believe. Maybe the journey went by quickly because I had Mitchell's practical spell lesson turning about in my mind. I suppose it was another method to get your own way through positive energy, rather than negative. We reached the entrance to The Oracle Farm just off the main road. A slight *farmy* smell wafted out to greet us but that soon mixed in with petrol and factory fumes from the town, stagnating it instantly. Inside the grey mesh gates, my ears were confronted with animal noises – bleating, neighing and honking mixed up into a chorus of discordant farm songs. There were fenced-off pasture areas of goats and geese. Next to them, a group of inquisitive llamas who poked their heads over their enclosure to observe some playful pigs with an old tyre and a football. A large reception building stood proudly, bearing a shiny plaque over its entrance:

The Oracle Farm is part of a community charity set up five years ago to connect the community with nature. The three-and-a-half-acre site containing animal pastures and vegetable and fruit gardens provides an educational programme to schools as well as work experience for young people, all supported by the London Boroughs Trust. We thank all those volunteers involved in running the farm and for all their fundraising efforts to keep our precious farm alive.

Ahead of that was a gravel path overshadowed either side by fruit trees. It was weird being in the heart of London yet seeing a couple of acres of trees around us. City buildings towered over us like Lego blocks; the many windows within them looked like black square holes. My mouth became strangely dry as I turned from the beautiful trees ahead of me to the lack of colour behind, as if it was being swallowed up. A constant drone from traffic whirred in my ears, making me feel slightly queasy.

A large blackboard greeted us with a whole load of information chalked upon it in white. Plant-based cooking workshop; poster design class; vegetable planting garden; teaching rooms…although some previous visitor had found a permanent fluorescent pink marker to make it into teaching **b**rooms instead.

"Okay, class," began Mitchell. "This is where we begin. Year 12 are waiting for you in the dining area, but first Mrs

Webster, who runs The Oracle Farm, wants to say a few words."

Mrs Webster was dressed in jeans and a worn-looking navy-blue anorak, together with muddy wellington boots that came up to her knees. She wore no make-up and wasn't bad-looking exactly but her dark, bushy eyebrows made her appear quite a bit like a man. She smiled broadly, revealing a big gap in the front of her teeth, instantly demoting her status from *not bad-looking* to *wicked witch with possible warts*.

"Welcome, everyone. It's lovely to have you here," she lisped. "It's so important to have this green area in a city that envelopes so much of Mother Nature. It's a little hidden oasis in a desert of pollution."

"That's a nice way to put it," whispered Thomas. "Mind you, judging by the colour of the sky, I'd say we'd need a whole lot more oasises."

"It's oases," I responded, gazing up at the sky, a blank grey, stretching endlessly across the city. He had a point.

"After lunch you can take a look around and familiarise yourselves with our friendly animals – pigs, chickens, a couple of goats – to name but a few. Please be considerate to other visitors. We have many school parties here so bear in mind that we are a small concern and must compromise with space. We must also show respect for our animal friends. Keep the noise to a reasonable level. Don't unnerve them. You may pet them but there is no maltreatment here. We are all equal beings. After you've familiarised yourselves with the farm, I'll take you to our vegetable gardens where you'll learn about soil and planting and the importance of sharing our proceeds as well as the ill effects of wasting. To quote

Gandhi: *The world has enough for everyone's needs, but not everyone's greed*. We'll teach you how to distribute your leftover fruit and veg. There are now a huge number of food-sharing schemes around. We operate a volunteer scheme with our produce whereby volunteers offer their time, digging beds, sowing seeds or harvesting fruit and vegetables in return for a bag of local farm-grown seasonal stuff to take home. We also have a wormery here for upcycling rinds, peels, stalks and cores.

"That sounds disgusting," whispered Letty.

Our teachers chatted with Mrs Webster and followed her inside, leaving us to wash our hands and freshen up before going in for lunch.

The canteen-style dining room with painted sunshines, flowers and frogs all over the walls was bright and welcoming. Quinton Earth Science School Year 12 students sat at metal tables pushed together, accompanied by uncomfortable-looking metal chairs, probably digging into every part of their bodies that shouldn't be dug into. Fresh crusty rolls, resembling rocks in tatty old baskets were scattered along each table, smelling surprisingly better than they looked. An oldish-looking bearded man wearing a white turban, a cream jumper and navy jeans, spoke to three or four of the students on the Year 12 table.

"Who's that?" asked Letty, her face crimson.

"That's Guru Aabavaana," replied Myerscough.

"Not *him*," whispered Letty in my ear. "I meant the boy sitting on his right."

"That's Ashkii Mitchell," I said, with a snigger.

"Mitchell's son?"

I nodded.

"He's gorgeous," she whispered again.

The guru acknowledged Myerscough with a nod, then turned to me offering a gesture of namaste and a smile, which I returned. Myerscough pushed me into the seat beside the guru, making a disgruntled Year 12 girl get up and move somewhere else. Myerscough sat next to me on the other side, making me feel like part of a *loser* sandwich.

The farm laid on a special vegan meal for us – ratatouille Bolognese.

"What's ratted tooey?" asked Thomas, who'd sat opposite me.

"It's a French stewed vegetable dish – not usually served with pasta, and not normally associated with Bolognese," I replied, not bothering to correct his pronunciation as the food approached the table: a mass of soggy vegetables in a gooey tomato sauce, dolloped onto mushy pasta. It looked more like *rat's-gooey-spewy*.

"Ellery, I'd like you to meet Guru Aabavaana. He's been working with Quinton students on and off for many years. He's a wise man. You should pay attention."

I said nothing as I took a hard bread roll in favour of the rat vomit.

"Good to meet you, Ellery," began the guru in an unexpectedly broad Welsh accent. Practically his whole face was taken up by a beard with matching silvery eyebrows. A sort of dark-skinned Father Christmas with a turban. His hazel eyes were mischievous but honest. I read somewhere that your eyes were the window to your soul. If that were true, then I'd have to say Guru Aabavaana's soul was definitely smiling. He carried an air of peace and calm, just like Dave

73

used to. As he chatted to Myerscough, I let his calming voice wash over me.

"Vegan pudding!" shouted a woman from behind the counter.

Thomas's eyes lit up as he shot off his chair to see what was on offer. He returned less enthusiastic with a single banana on his plate.

"It might seem like a poor effort to you here," started the guru, "but this farm has done great things in a very short space of time. Planting trees and growing crops, saving animals from many unmentionable atrocities. One has to start somewhere. I think they hope that by teaching the young to be different, the young will pass it on to their parents to be different too. A big ask, don't you think?" He looked over at Letty, who wasn't listening, too busy drooling over Ashkii Mitchell. I nudged her.

"Yes," agreed Letty, obviously completely unaware of what she was agreeing with.

The guru paused and raised his eyebrows, two hairy caterpillars meeting up in the middle of his forehead.

"It can't be up to just Magaecians to save the world," added Delia.

"Exactly," said the guru. "We must work together. It should be up to everybody. After all, we are all part of Magae. No matter if you are Dweller or Magaecian, your body is a piece of her – made up of water, minerals and elements. She has always taken care of us, so it's time we took care of her."

"What will happen if we don't?" asked Thomas, munching on his banana.

"Then she will have to do everything in her power to save herself," answered the guru. "You must not forget that life on Magae is not just human life, but all life. We must stop thinking that we are the most important all of the time. If humans disappeared from Magae, she would still flourish – but if a species like the earthworm, for example, disappeared, an important creature that protects our soil, pushing up nutrients to make it fertile, then life might vanish faster than you think. We would end up with less food, more floods and more pollution. Even worm poo is packed with beneficial nutrients for plants." He smiled, observing Thomas's giggly reaction to the words *worm poo*.

"So how will we make things better?" asked Delia.

"I'm not sure I know the answer unless human beings begin to recognise that we need to preserve all life on Magae, not just our own species. It's not about making *our* lives better but about saving *all* life on our planet…before it is too late and Magae can bear us no longer. I'm afraid it might take a disaster before man wakes up to this plight."

"Will Magae wipe us all out?" asked Nyle.

"Magae will make things better for herself. I'm not sure she'll completely wipe us out, but perhaps she will reduce our numbers. Our population is too many. Magae does not have enough resources for all of us."

"But that's terrible," said Letty, now completely engaged in the debate.

"You are seeing it as a catastrophe, but perhaps it should be viewed as a solution. Although humans are awesome, maybe Magae is unable to cope with so much awesomeness. I mean, we can travel the world, to any place at any time with no difficulty. We can want something we see on the internet and have it in our hand the next day. We can remove disease and prolong life. We can change nature by genetically modifying her, but we are reaching the point where we have become so disconnected from her that we risk becoming incompatible with her. We are too much. We need to be less. To survive we need to appreciate the life Magae freely gives us. We would not exist without her fresh air, running water…"

"Trees!" shouted Thomas. "We need more trees."

"Yes, young man. We do," said the guru, pointing at Thomas. "Trees are the lungs of Magae. The stuff they breathe out, we breathe in. The stuff we breathe out, they breathe in. We cannot do without them. As long as you want to keep breathing, you need to keep trees."

"So if everyone plants a tree, we'd be okay?" asked Thomas.

"If everyone plants a tree, we might stand a chance," replied the guru, touching his bushy beard.

"Quinton School!" blasted out of some speakers hanging precariously from the corner of the room. "We'll be ready for you to start some fruit and vegetable picking in fifteen minutes. If you want to take a little wander around, you should do so now, please. We'll wait for you outside the reception building."

Loud screeches of metal chairs simultaneously pushing back to release uncomfortable Year 9 and Year 12 bottoms filled the air like an orchestra out of tune. We disposed of our dirty plates, then headed outside.

"Thank you, Aab," said Myerscough, shaking hands

with Guru Aabavaana, after removing the chair which had got locked onto his large thighs.

Outside, there were a couple of groups of kids from different schools. None of them acknowledged us, almost ignoring our presence completely. From the corner of my eye I noticed a lonely figure, sitting on the grassy bank near the farm souvenir shop. It was Orford. I'm not sure how long he'd been there. In fact, I reckon he'd skipped lunch.

"I'll catch you up," I said to the others who were heading for the pig pen. I climbed the bank and sat next to Orford. "You okay?"

"Sure," he replied, shrugging his shoulders, staring at nothing.

"You seem quiet," I tried again.

"Do I?"

"Orford, these one-word answers are very unhelpful."

"*Do I*, is two words, Ellery." He paused for a moment. "Look, it's nothing. Just leave me alone. It's complicated."

"Perhaps I can help," I offered.

"Perhaps you can mind your own business," he retorted.

"Fine." As I got up to leave, Orford gasped.

"*Hell!* Where did they come from?"

"Who?" I replied, following Orford's gaze in an attempt to work out where he was looking and who had spooked him so much. He'd focused on three suited men, heading towards the farm entrance. One, unmistakably the ex-Circle member, Gibson Hastings. The tall skinny frame, the steely grey hair, that dreadful gaunt face. But why was he here?

"Orford – what's going on?" I demanded.

"There's no time to explain. You wouldn't understand, anyway. I've got to get out of here." He slid down the bank and ran into the souvenir shop, ducking behind a crate of pink and white llama toys.

I followed. "I'll keep watch," I whispered.

I peered through the half-open window. The men were heading this way, for the farm shop. I ducked, crawling on my stomach to join Orford behind the crate, which was directly under the window. Their footsteps grew nearer and so did their voices. Right by the window. Beads of sweat trickled down Orford's face and settled on his eyebrows as he held his breath. They were right above us. If they turned around and glanced through the window, we'd be discovered. For a fraction of a second I thought it was all over but then they moved away. I glimpsed through the window to see them heading towards the reception building like a trio of clones, identical from the back. All the same height, in the same suits, walking in perfect step with one another.

"Too close," puffed Orford. "Let's get out of here."

"We should find Myerscough or Mitchell. Those men wouldn't dare touch you while you're with *them*."

Orford nodded, then slowly ventured out of the shop with me trailing behind looking left and right. It was all going well until Thomas screamed out, "Ellery! Orford! You coming to pick fruit?"

We both winced and turned like a pair of synchronised dancers to spot all three men turn away from the reception doorway like a pack of wolves suddenly catching a waft of prey in the breeze. Orford froze as the men bolted down the path, making a beeline for him.

"Get Myerscough!" I screamed to Thomas, then grabbed Orford by the wrist and sprinted away with him. We headed to the fruit trees and dodged our way through them, getting slashed by overhanging branches. Orford seemed to accelerate so I forced myself to run faster too. As we tried to put some distance between us and the men, I thought my lungs might burst. Choking, sweating, Orford whirled to the side, to miss one of the men who'd caught up and lunged for him. The man missed, stumbled hard and landed on his stomach with a thump. Orford ran so fast I couldn't keep up. I tired and I lost my concentration as it dawned on me that I didn't even know why we were running in the first place. I tripped on some tree roots but luckily managed to regain my balance to continue onwards. The orchard ended with a low stone wall, separating the trees from the vegetables. It was easy to straddle over; Orford took it like an Olympic hurdler. Neither of us risked looking back over our shoulders for the men. We sprinted through the vegetables, arms pumping. I wondered whether Orford's lungs were burning as much as mine. The earth here was squelchy and seemed to grasp at my ankles, pulling me down, trying to suck me into the roots. I slipped on the mud and tasted a mouthful of mouldy soil. I scrambled to my feet but slipped again. Orford turned back, offering a hand. We sprinted on but it was hopeless; ahead of us was an abrupt end, a kind of courtyard. Standing proudly in the middle of it, in fact, sticking out like a sore thumb, was a very large fountain. It was the type you'd normally see in a massive shopping centre or maybe in the gardens of a stately home – definitely not in a little city farm. Ahead of that stood a two-metre-high brick wall and no way of getting over it. We were trapped.

We ran behind the monster of a fountain, numerous jets spraying up several metres into the air to cascade down into a large pool like a watery willow tree. We dived for cover behind it, ducking as near to the ground as we could, waiting a few minutes before peering over the lip of the fountain bowl. The men hammered through the vegetable gardens, like human bulldozers, surging ever closer, hunting with malice. We'd put a little distance between us and them but they'd inevitably find us. I mean, where else could we have gone but behind the fountain? I looked across at Orford, his face a flood of panic. He emptied his pockets, revealing a packet of sweets and two totem stones – a lizard and a bat.

"What are you doing?" I gasped, trying to catch my breath.

"I'm calling on my totems for help. You should do the same."

I reached into my pocket too. I pulled out my honey badger totem stone, still smelling faintly of mint. I didn't want to call my totem in case I summoned the dragon instead. A surge of panic hit me like a punch. I wished I'd never gone back to school but had stayed in Tribourne with Mum and Lionel.

"Blast them with pain!" cried Orford, his gaze frantic. "You're an ebonoid, aren't you?"

An avalanche of gunshots perforated the fountain, blasting chips of stone and water into the air over our heads. These men were trying to kill us. What on earth could Orford have done? I choked back the bile rising in my throat. My body jolted with every new shot fired. I didn't want to die, hunted down in this way. This wasn't the ending I'd imagined. I thought I was meant to be special. I thought I was meant to be the one to finish what Darwin Burgess had started. I suppose the only reality that faced me now was that I hadn't a clue what to do. I'd never had a clue what to do and probably never would. I'd *have* to turn on these men and use my negative power like Orford said. I knew I shouldn't, but what other choice did I have? Orford was rooted to the spot, his totem stones in each trembling hand and his face as pale as a corpse. As I stood up to face the enemy, a huge wave of water smashed over me, knocking me off my feet as if I'd been hit by a bus. The fountain pedestal collapsed in another deluge of gunshots. Water gushed everywhere like a surging torrent. Gasping and spluttering to catch my breath between violent coughs and gurgles, my tongue became suddenly tingly. I'm not totally sure what happened next, all I know is that I somehow "grabbed" the pumping water in my hands and "pushed" it like a solid block. It flew torpedo-style at the men, pinning one to the wall in front of the orchard, and forcefully overcoming the other two who ended up splayed out, face down, guns sunk fast into the mud.

"Get up!" demanded Myerscough, running to Gibson Hastings, aggressively grabbing him by the scruff of the neck. Myerscough could be frightening if you got on the wrong side of him. My heart thumped hard in my chest and I couldn't stop my teeth from chattering. Mitchell strode elegantly to the scene, followed by a young, skinny workman from the farm. They took the other two men, frogmarching them to the reception building where a number of police cars had gathered. I suspect Mrs Webster must have called them.

As I tried to make sense of what had just happened, Orford stood mute, his mouth gaping wide. He looked like a crazy person. I think he was in shock.

6

THE DRAGON'S GUIDE

Orford and I missed the fruit and vegetable picking, too busy drying out and warming up. Our classmates had managed to fill two large canvas bags with fresh produce, all shapes and sizes. Nothing genetically modified into the perfect stuff in supermarkets. My teeth chattered so much my jaw ached. Orford, on the other hand, looked as though he'd recovered, but he did seem subdued.

"Your lips are blue," said Thomas.

"Here." Myerscough handed me a cup of hot chocolate from a flask in his rucksack. My arctic insides slowly defrosted as the velvety drink warmed and soothed my shaking body. I needed to know why those men had tried to kill Orford, but he was busy answering questions from Mr Mitchell. I decided to leave my own questioning until later. I didn't have the energy.

"You okay?" asked Nyle, walking out of the farm gates with me.

I nodded with a smile.

"What was that all about?"

"I don't know," I replied, teeth still chattering a little.

"I'll find out for you. Leave it to me."

I nodded, then changed the subject. "Where are we going now?"

"Back to Quinton."

"Not walking, are we? I'm exhausted."

"I think so. Anyway, Chef MacBrennan's making us dinner before we go off tonight."

"Off where?"

"To Aberdeen...not walking, of course." Nyle laughed. "We're getting the overnight train from Euston. Should be fun. I've never slept on a train before. What about you?"

"Aberdeen? Like Scotland, Aberdeen?" I replied, ignoring his question.

"Yeah. We're not actually staying in Aberdeen – that's just as far as the train goes. I think we're getting a ferry from there to the Isle of Sealgair."

"The Isle of where?" I asked.

"Sealgair. You were busy getting shot at when Mr Ademola arrived to tell us all about it. It's a little Scottish island. He said our school uses an old ski resort there, *The Palace*, abandoned, because the effects of global warming mean there's not enough snow for paying customers."

"Right." I nodded. I suppose sleeping on a train sounded kind of fun, not that I'd be able to sleep – not with a dragon trying to kill me and a smelly worm to vomit me to death. The thought of throwing up on a train made me queasy. It gave me an idea, though. I could read my way through the night with some totem books from the Quinton library. That would definitely keep me awake.

***

After Chef MacBrennan's wonderful smoky cauliflower steaks, followed by home-grown apple crumble from the Quinton orchard, I ran to the library to find relevant totem books, trying to avoid the super-heavy volumes, instead going for the concise, pocket books. The rest of my class had already assembled outside Quinton House. It was just before half past seven, and the sun was dipping, sending a fiery orange along the horizon, like a battle signal behind the skyline of London buildings. I watched my shadow shrink, disappearing under my feet.

We got the tube to Euston station, which was only a couple of stops away. I could see why it was known to be one of the busiest stations in Britain. A fast-flowing river of humans confronted us, like a seething mass, shoulder to shoulder. Strange how such a crowd of people can become faceless objects in your way. Myerscough shepherded us to the right platform where a large shiny train waited patiently for passengers. Mitchell sorted out our carriages with an official-looking person in a navy and red uniform, then signalled for Myerscough to lead us on.

"There's a bunk bed in each cabin, so pair up, please," yelled Myerscough, striding onto the train as if there were no large steps, unlike the rest of us who needed to hold the metal railing on the side for the climb up.

Letty and I grabbed each other, Kemp and Thomas agreed to pair up and Nyle said he'd go with Orford, who was at the back of the line. Nyle and I had agreed on our walk back to Quinton that we had a mission to find out from Orford why the old Magaecian Circle were trying to kill him.

"Wow!" squealed Letty, opening our cabin door. "This is so cool. It's like being in a hotel."

The room was very narrow but housed a large, silver bunk bed, covered in crisp white linen. Extra blue fleece blankets lay folded on the top of each bed.

"Top or bottom?" asked Letty, throwing down her bag and leaping up to the top.

"Bottom," I answered, knowing she'd struggle to fold her long lanky body into the lower bunk.

"Thanks. I was hoping you'd say that."

There were all sorts of switches and sockets for music and phones and stuff. There was even a little sink containing two white flannels and two bottles of mineral water.

"Not very eco-friendly," said Letty, eyeing the plastic bottles.

"What's this?" I said, picking up two blue bags. I passed one to Letty to open.

"It's free soap." She laughed. "Oooh, and there are some earplugs and an eye mask. Cool."

Myerscough peeped his head round the door. "There's a room service menu, should you need to buy anything during the night," he said, waving a little booklet about. "Don't go ordering wine or whisky unless you want a month of detention. I've organised breakfast to be brought to your rooms at 6am. We arrive in Aberdeen around 7:20

so make sure you're awake and ready, please. There's a shower down the hall if you're feeling brave and a toilet a couple of doors along. Lights out at ten at the latest. Sleep well."

Letty and I looked at each other with the same thought in mind – the boys. We waited a little while to make sure Myerscough had gone, then left our cabin with our credit card-type key and knocked on a few doors until we found the right cabin. Thomas let us in, then jumped on the lower bunk. Kemp climbed down the ladder from the top bunk to join him. We entered single file. It was a tight fit.

"Are you going to tell us what happened at the farm, Ellery? I mean, why were those men shooting at you?" asked Thomas, rubbing his hands together, as if I must have enjoyed the experience.

"It wasn't me they were shooting at. I think it was Orford."

"Orford?" shouted Kemp.

"Shhhhh!" I put my finger to my lips.

"Why Orford?" continued Kemp more quietly.

"I don't know. Nyle's going to try to find out. He's sharing a room with him." I paused for a minute then added, "I know what Orford's new totem is, by the way."

"Really?" said Letty. "What?"

"It's a bat."

"Bats are meant to help you focus, aren't they?" said Letty.

"They're creatures of the night. Don't they signal the end?" added Kemp, chewing the inside of his mouth.

"The end of what?" I asked.

"You mean death?" whispered Thomas, his eyebrows almost disappearing under his curly hair.

No one said anything. We just looked at each other in silence.

"Wait," said Kemp, his finger raised. "I've just thought of something."

"What?" said Letty.

"It's not good."

"What?" repeated Letty, her voice lashing at him like a whip.

"If Orford's totems are a bat and a lizard, then – if you put them together... I mean, what would you get if you crossed a bat with a lizard?"

"A blizzard?" answered Thomas.

Letty let out a burst of giggles. Mine was more of a nervous laugh; I knew what Kemp was inferring.

"You're thinking *dragon*, aren't you?" I said.

Kemp nodded.

"Of course," said Letty. "I didn't think of that. Do you think it's Orford's dragon that you've been seeing when you call your totem?"

"Do you think Orford's trying to kill you?" asked Thomas, his eyes darting between me and Kemp.

"No. That's the thing," I replied. "I *don't* think he's trying to kill me. I really don't."

"What can it mean?" asked Letty.

"Can we think about it tomorrow?" said Thomas, stretching out onto the bed. "I'm pooped."

"He's right," I agreed. "Let's go back before the teachers catch us out of our room."

Letty and I went back to our cabin. We chatted for a short time but Letty nodded off quite quickly. I was exhausted and my feet were aching – we'd walked miles and miles today. I closed my eyes but it was no use, I couldn't get to sleep; my mind was wide awake. I couldn't stop thinking about how I'd almost got shot this afternoon, and how I'd swallowed practically the entire contents of a fountain the size of Buckingham Palace. I sat up. I reached over to get out the Quinton library books from my bag and began my research. I put on the reading light above the bed but it wasn't really bright enough to see clearly. I took the card-key, put the books in my rucksack and left the room with it for a brighter area of the train. I suppose I could have sat in the loo but it wasn't the most pleasant smelling of areas so I headed for the buffet car which only contained a couple of people. The lighting was bright there. I walked through to take a seat with a table by the window. I stared outside, watching only blackness, only shadows of faraway trees passing by in a forest swallowed up by darkness. I felt suddenly like the world was closing in on me. As I surrounded myself with totem books and notes, I couldn't remove an impending doom distracting me. The words on the page began to wobble and made no sense as they danced around mocking me. I began to shiver.

"Can't sleep?" Guru Aabavaana appeared from nowhere with a plate of chips. He sat down opposite me.

I smiled.

"Sometimes, my eyes are bigger than my stomach. You might have to help me with these," he said, pushing the plate into the middle of the table. I took a couple. "What are you reading?" he continued.

I slid one of the books towards him, a dragon totem drawing and its meaning splashed over a double page.

"I see. Dragons. Fascinating. Do you know much about them?"

"Not really, sir."

"It's a bit like Top Trumps. Ever played?"

"Sure," I replied, remembering the *Star Wars* ones I had at home.

"Well, the dragon totem is like the mother lode of all trump cards, the best card, unbeatable – except..." He paused for a moment.

"Except what, sir?"

"Except, like all good trump cards, there is always one weakness on the card that might enable someone else to take it from you. That's why a dragon totem nearly always comes with a guide."

"What do you mean, sir?"

"Well..." he began. "Dragons are said to be Magae's spirit animal, and as such are difficult to handle. Such a tremendous energy, they are masters of the elements. They need to have their power transferred to the surface of the world. They are a warrior totem to bring back balance to the elemental forces. Used wisely they will offer courage and strength. They are a symbol of peace but without a guide, it is too easy to let one's ego take charge. One must not use its energy foolishly, without discretion. The dragon will protect you when you use its energy for greater good, but it's a whole other story when you hunger for its power only for greed. Ignore guidance and the consequences can be costly."

We sat quietly for a few minutes. Perhaps I was the guide and Orford was the dragon. Maybe that's why they were after him. If Nash had returned, then he'd want the dragon totem. He must've misused its power when he was young and lost it, and now he wanted it back. Perhaps it was up to me to protect Orford. My thoughts were interrupted by Aab's loud munching.

"What if the guide's frightened of the dragon?" I asked.

The guru stroked his beard. "You would be a fool not to fear it. They are hostile and threatening but the guide must find a way to connect with it, to approach it. I would suggest thinking without your senses. Remove yourself from sight, sound, taste, smell and touch and just connect with your life force, your living energy so that you feel through Magae's senses instead of your own. The dragon will relate to this."

"Nash had a dragon totem, didn't he, sir?"

"Yes, he did. Being ebonoid, he needed a guide more than most but he chose not to listen." Aab looked into the distance as if to recall something in his past. "It is probably why Nash's totem became a snake. Snakes and dragons are very closely tied in legend, you know? They have an affinity to the life-giving energy of Magae."

"You mean, his totem wasn't always a snake, sir?" I asked.

"No, this was not his natural totem."

"What was it, then, sir?"

"I think it was a worm."

7

THE ISLE OF SEALGAIR

Our arrival in Aberdeen and subsequent ferry to Sealgair was a bit of a blur. Thoughts following my chat with Aab tore through my head like a tornado. I was in a daze for most of the journey until the sea became a bit choppy and prompted me to venture up the ferry stairs for some air.

"What's up?" asked Nyle, following me.

"Nothing. I think I'm a bit seasick. Did you find anything out from Orford?"

"Useless."

"What are you two doing up here? Having a snog?" asked Orford, who had come up behind us on the stairs.

"No!" snapped Nyle, looking very red in the face. "She's feeling seasick. She doesn't need your help."

"Actually," I said, "I think we need to talk."

"About what?" said Orford, a slight tone of indifference detectable in his voice.

"You must have some idea why those men tried to kill you?"

"Not really. Mum told me, the first day of school in Butterly's office, that I should keep away from *the ebonoid*." He gestured with inverted commas in the air.

"And that was it?"

Orford looked at the floor and shrugged.

That obviously wasn't it but it was also obvious he wasn't going to say any more. I'd have to think of another way to find out.

"The thing is, Orford," I began, "I think your totems combine to make a dragon."

"What?"

"A bat and a lizard – together, they make a dragon, don't they?"

Orford cracked his knuckles. Nyle folded his arms across his body.

"A dragon has legendary power, elemental forces that Nash once had but misused and lost. He sees you as another chance to get back that power, don't you see? Aab told me last night that dragons always come with a guide. They're too powerful to handle alone."

"What are you on about?" he said, shrugging with open hands.

"I think I'm your guide. Perhaps your mum wanted you to stay away from me because I'm the only one that can stop Nash from taking your dragon. It has to be."

"That doesn't make sense," replied Orford, eyes narrowed. "If he wants my dragon, then why would he try to kill me? He won't get it if I'm dead. Shouldn't he try to kill you?"

"He's got a point," added Nyle.

"Maybe *I'm* the guide," said Orford, raising his eyebrows with a smile. "It would make more sense. I mean, that's why he'd want me out of the way…to stop me from protecting *your* dragon."

"That's ridiculous," yelled Nyle. "She doesn't have a dragon."

"She doesn't have a honey badger either, so I hear," added Orford.

"Who told you that?" I squawked, clenching my jaws together, wondering if I'd ever find anyone that could keep a secret for more than five minutes.

"It's hardly a secret that you might be an elemental."

"What's that supposed to mean?" I snapped back, assuming he must be throwing some sort of Magaecian insult at me.

"An elemental," repeated Orford. "An ebonoid with a dragon totem will be able to produce elemental energy physically – like you produce your negative energy."

"I don't understand."

"I do," said Nyle. "That gust of wind that saved us in the Quinton House tunnel – I thought that was luck but…"

"And the fountain fiasco?" added Orford. "How do you think that water blasted those men?"

"What? That's ludicrous," I shouted. "That wasn't me."

"What's ludicrous?" asked Thomas, who had joined us with Letty and Kemp, pushing his head between us.

"I'm not the one with the dragon totem," began Orford. "It's *her*."

"So you're the guide?" asked Kemp, directing his question at Orford.

"Totally Hawk!" squealed Thomas.

"I doubt it," replied Orford, ignoring Thomas's outburst.

"It's simple." Letty nodded, her eyes darting wildly between Orford and me. "You've got to approach that dragon you keep seeing, Ellery, and Orford's got to be there to guide you."

Nyle's face twitched.

"Guide her?" said Orford, turning purple. "I'm no guide. I mean, I haven't got a clue what a guide should do. Talk about it with Mitchell or Guru Aabavaana, not me. I can't help you."

"He's right," agreed Nyle.

"No, I don't think we should tell anyone else. Not yet, anyway. Not until we're absolutely sure about this."

Nyle forced a smile which looked more like a wild animal baring its teeth.

***

The chilly air on the Isle of Sealgair didn't deter the many seagulls from dive-bombing us near the water. A large sign with a red circle and a picture of a bag of chips with a line through it took my attention.

"Do you think it's illegal to eat chips here?" asked Thomas, scrunching up his nose.

"Seagulls love chips," Myerscough said, laughing. "They're notorious for pinching people's food. The residents of Sealgair don't want to encourage them to depend on human food. It makes them quite aggressive."

The thought of food made my stomach rumble. I'd hardly touched my breakfast and that was hours ago.

"School's just up there," said Myerscough, pointing to a mountain in the distance. "We'll be taking the cable car. It doesn't take long."

Thomas bounced up and down, a wide grin spread across his face.

We split into groups and rode up the mountain in small cable cars, also known as mountain gondolas according to Delia. I think they must have been used to transfer skiers to the slopes when they had more snow. A small, rectangular information notice above one of the seats read:

Welcome to Mount Ghuthan, also known as the "Mountain of Voices". This is due to the conversational twittering which sounds like many voices, produced by the large population of goldfinches that reside here. Listen and you'll hear them! Of course, some think the voices belong to the lost souls of Manburgh. Those that die on the mountain are cursed to remain on the mountain forever.

Manburgh? I wondered where that was. Squinting through the brightness of the sun, brilliant against the glass, I absorbed the stunning view, like a journey to the clouds. It's how I imagined the Alps might be. Mount Ghuthan rose steeply and dramatically into the heavens, taking my breath away. Blinded briefly, my eyes watering from the sun's intensity, I turned away, snatching a peek of the valley below. An enchanting little village. A small fairy-tale-like church – at least it seemed small from up here – surrounded by pretty cottages with red-bricked chimneys, creating a serene landscape among the gold and red autumn trees.

"I'm starving," announced Thomas, rubbing his stomach.

We arrived at the old hotel, now our school for the next three terms. It might have been called *The Palace* but it looked more like a worn-out fortress. I reckon the whole of Tribourne Village could have fitted inside its walls. High, forbidding, turreted walls which didn't scream *fun holiday location* to me. It must have been hundreds of years old, probably with a violent history of sieges and clan battles to go with it. A sign pointed to the *Manburgh Cemetery*, definitely not something you'd want adjoining your school, or your hotel for that matter. Mum always described cemeteries as places of rest and peace; I thought they were places of ghosts and all things demonic and creepy. I shuddered, looking up at the long spires of the building piercing the sky, like crooked needles. Eerie gargoyles perched intermittently, frowning at our arrival. Judging by the look on my friends' faces, I don't think I was the only one feeling unwelcome. A huge gate, topped with sharp metal spikes led through to an enormous archway and cobbled courtyard. Disregarded skis and an abandoned snow plough were just a few reminders of its tourist days. An uneasiness passed through me, forcing me to conclude that the lack of snow was probably not the only reason customers kept away. We entered the courtyard, faced with a statuesque water feature of a lady staring skywards, her mouth open to release a fountain of water, I suspect, but her lips were dry, green and mouldy as were her cracked hands. I don't suppose it had been working for years. It sent an instant shiver through me. After yesterday, another fountain was the last thing I wanted to see.

"Welcome, Year 9s. I'm Mr Lameko. I will be teaching you foraging spells this term. However, today, I am your tour guide. Let's get some refreshments, then I'll take you around *The Palace*."

Mr Lameko, average height and quite thickset, wore a long skirt and a profusion of women's jewellery. His shoulder-length hair, thick and luscious, framed his broad face, which was smooth and sculpted.

"Is he a man or a woman?" whispered Thomas.

"He's a dyad, you silly," whispered Nyle, behind me.

"What's a dyad?" I asked.

"You know? Undivided."

I shook my head.

"*Esprit unis*. Joined spirits?"

I shook my head again.

"Male and female together. Like a third gender."

"Do you mean transgender?" I asked.

"Similar," said Nyle. "In Magaecian culture, a dyad is someone who embodies the spirit of both female and male. They don't try to be one or the other, they simply embrace both."

"We see them as valued members of our society," added Delia, who'd obviously felt the need to add her knowledge with a little dig at Dwellers' behaviour. "Being able to nurture both feminine and masculine spirits makes them better as teachers and healers. More caring as they possess gifts of man and woman."

"That's lovely," said Letty, sounding a little bit stupid, but in truth, she was right. It *was* lovely. It made me realise how unnecessarily judgemental Dwellers could be and how glad I felt to be part of the Magaecian community and culture.

We followed Mr Lameko, who led us through the courtyard and out onto a green area where stood a ruined church and cemetery.

"This is the Manburgh Church and abbey," said Lameko, pointing to the roofless building, which was just a shell really with weeds growing through it.

"Most of it was demolished in 1800," he continued, leading us past it. "Down here, these old buildings are out of bounds. They were the old cells, of course. You're not to go messing about round there, do you understand?"

"Cells?" I blurted out far too loudly.

"When it was a prison in the early 1900s."

"A prison?" squealed Thomas, who'd become so pale his freckles stood out proudly from his white complexion as if they were about to drop off his face and onto the floor.

"I thought it was an old hotel," said Nyle. "*The Palace*."

"Haha! Your teachers have been playing tricks on you." Lameko chuckled. "*The Palace* is a sarcastic nickname for Manburgh Prison. Anything but a palace, I'm afraid."

"Is it haunted?" asked Letty, her words flying out like they were burning her tongue.

"Some say it is," Lameko replied, with a wink and a smirk. "The main building's used regularly for weddings and other functions, so don't worry, your bedrooms will be far from an unpleasant prison cell." He laughed again, obviously finding our reactions highly amusing. "Let's eat. You'll need your strength to explore the grounds afterwards," he said, leading us towards the main building.

"A prison," said Kemp, his voice high and shrill. "No one told us we'd be in a prison."

I admit, a prison was a daunting thought, but I had other things on my mind. I had an urgent need to confront this dragon and get it over with. I grabbed Orford by the arm.

"Let's meet tonight with our totems. I've got to know if I really am the dragon."

"Okay," he returned. "But I'm telling you now, I'm not your guide."

"I think we should be there too," said Nyle. "A dragon's a lot to handle if things get out of hand."

I nodded. Kemp, Letty and Thomas didn't look so keen.

"Where shall we meet?" asked Nyle.

"How about the haunted prison cells?" answered Orford, raising up one eyebrow.

"Count me out," spat Kemp.

"Me too," added Letty.

"It's out of bounds. You can't meet there anyway," said Thomas. "You'll get in trouble."

"We'll have to use the cemetery," I said. As soon as the words left my lips, I wanted to catch them and put them straight back into my mouth, but it was too late.

"Good idea. I'm in," said Orford. "What about you, scaredy-pants?" he sniggered at Kemp.

"He's not scared, he just doesn't want to get into trouble," said Letty.

Kemp smiled at Letty's lame attempt to stick up for him, then turned to Orford. "Sure. No problem, mate."

"Isn't there anywhere else we could meet?" said Thomas, his eyebrows knitting together, probably and understandably trying to come up with somewhere less creepy. "I mean, what if someone's visiting a grave or something?"

"At night – in the dark?" shrieked Orford.

"Just saying," said Thomas, his face turning crimson.

"If you're too much of a chicken, then stay in your bedroom and play with your teddies," answered Orford, with a sarcastic smile.

"I'm not scared," snapped Thomas, his complexion now ruddier than ever. "I was just worried about everyone else, that's all."

"Of course you were," sniggered Orford, raising his eyebrows.

✳✳✳

We agreed to meet at midnight in the Year 12 boys' toilets, which were on the other side of the building to the teachers' bedrooms, according to Kemp. Apparently, this was to "give the older students some responsibility and independence". I reckon the *older students* needed far more supervision than the younger students. Anyway, Kemp was right; the toilets were where he said they would be, but I'm not sure how we'd managed to get to them without waking everyone up – Thomas kept farting.

"Sorry," he whispered. "It always happens when I'm really nervous."

Orford puffed out his cheeks and shook his head in slow motion.

All the Year 12 boys' bedrooms and toilets were on the ground floor; the Year 12 girls were housed on the floor above. We tiptoed into the toilets to face six cubicles, each with a small window at the back. This was to be our escape route. We agreed to pair up, using three cubicles, in case anyone got stuck; getting through the window was going to be a tight squeeze.

No one got stuck as we landed on the grassy area outside, which was surrounded by a large prickly hedge. We found a small hole near the bottom of it, most likely made by foxes, or rabbits, which we slithered through on our stomachs. Letty got her hair caught on one of the prickles and lost quite a clump of it trying to untangle herself.

It was cold. I could hear the waves hissing along the shore as the wind grew harsh. Kemp looked as stiff as a poker.

"Are you okay?" I asked him.

"What if we get caught?" he whispered. "We'll be toast."

"I wish I had some toast," said Thomas, coming up behind us. "Covered in peanut butter and jam. I'm starving."

"After what's been firing from your backside?" said Orford. "Your fat bum's liable to catch fire."

"Oi!" returned Thomas indignantly.

"Well – I don't want you walking in front of me. Stay at the back – and try not to set the island alight."

"I've got a sensitive stomach," shouted Thomas, clenching both fists by his side.

"Yeh, right," answered Orford.

"Shush!" said Kemp, gnawing on his fist. "You're going to get us caught."

"We won't get caught," said Nyle. "Besides, there won't be any lights if we go the long way round through the trees and come up at the back of the abbey ruins."

"Go where and come up where? How do you even know this *long way round* exists?" demanded Kemp.

"Delia," replied Nyle, with a smug nod. "She asked Lameko, on our tour, how ancient residents of *The Palace* could have escaped unseen when they were under attack hundreds of years ago. He told her they would have taken the dark route."

"The dark route?" cried Thomas.

"Stop being such a wuss," shouted Orford.

"Stop making such a noise," said Kemp, shushing them both. "And stop wasting time. We need to get going."

I think we could all feel the rise of trepidation in our throats as we set off towards the trees; huge old oaks with thickened roots and cracked trunks. Their autumn leaves, now colourless silhouettes in the dark, rustled to sound like they were having a conversation in tree-language, whispering secrets between one another. In theory, according to Nyle, if we kept the lights from *The Palace* behind us, we wouldn't get lost – the *dark route* was meant to be a straight track. Nyle led the way, illuminating the path with his torch. We followed in silence, accompanied by the hooting of owls, hidden from view, until we reached a clearing, bringing us to the back of the abbey ruins. A surge of relief filled me from head to toe, soon replaced with a violent blast of terror, as a snapping twig cracked out like a shotgun to make me jump.

"I can see the cemetery," whispered Nyle.

A dog barked in the distance, alerting every nerve in my body as we walked together to the cemetery ahead. Long shadows followed us and a sense of unease hit me hard, telling me we shouldn't have come. The sight of the crumbling gravestones sent a prickle down my spine. Thomas's eyes darted from left to right as if the Grim Reaper might pop out to take him. "I can see why it's called a graveyard," he said, with a nervous giggle. "It's *grave* all right."

No one laughed. Now that the wind had died down it felt too quiet. A dreadful sinking feeling in my stomach made my hands go all shaky. I slammed them into my fleece pockets.

"Do you think the graves belong to old prisoners, hung for their crimes?" asked Thomas.

I reckon we were all asking the same question in our heads but nobody wanted to say it out loud. I wish he hadn't brought it up.

"Well, are we going to do this or not?" demanded Orford.

I nodded, although my insides screamed *turn back*.

"Let's sit against the wall of the old church," I said.

"Is that so nothing can come up behind us?" asked Thomas.

"Nothing's going to come up behind us," I shouted, without meaning to, but in truth, that's exactly what I was thinking.

We pulled off our jackets and rolled them up to act like seats to prevent our bottoms from getting wet on the damp grass.

"Okay, everyone got their totem stones out?" said Nyle, sounding like an orchestral conductor about to begin rehearsal.

The group nodded but I wasn't ready. I got up, taking a stone from in front of me, then sat down between my friends.

"What are you doing?" asked Letty.

"If I'm to find the dragon, then I need to leave the honey badger behind."

"But there's nothing on the stone," said Letty.

"I know. I'm going to try what Aab suggested. I'm going to give up my senses and feel through Magae's."

Letty nodded, seeming to agree with my idea.

"Ready?" I asked, clutching my new stone so tightly, any tighter and it could have crumbled to dust.

"Ready," replied Orford, a stone in each hand.

"Ready," repeated the others in unison.

I blocked out as many thoughts as I could and reached a meadow, green and calm. I entered a cave, blasted immediately by uncomfortably hot air. I squeezed my stone tighter. I sensed the dragon's presence, sucking the energy from my body with each thunderous heartbeat.

From the depths of the cave came a bat and a lizard. I guessed this to be Orford. Was he really my guide? He wasn't the mixture of bat and lizard that I'd expected. I felt a connection with Nyle's trusty dog, Kemp's mouse, Thomas's wild pig and Letty's heron which flew above us. Aab had told me on the train to let go of my senses and just *be*, feel Magae's senses instead of my own. It wasn't easy, taking a deep breath meant filling my lungs with the acrid air around me, most likely about to choke me. It was too late to chicken out now. Besides, dragons are meant to bring courage – so why did I feel so scared?

I needed to keep calm, but panic insisted on jabbing me hard in the stomach. My breathing quickened; my throat felt tight and clogged. My body became more and more stiff as if I were turning to stone. A terrible sense of impending doom paralysed me. I thought I might actually die. I wasn't feeling any of this so-called courage. In fact, at this point in time, all I felt was an almighty desire to turn back.

My breathing slowed and I focused on my friends' totems. These were animal spirits who had guided me last year, protecting me from Nash. I stopped shivering. My tongue tingled and a wave of power surged through me. Something stirred inside of me, through my veins. I forced my lungs to take in the biggest breath before surrendering myself to the dragon.

Searing pain overwhelmed me. I screamed out as my body rose upwards then smashed against something. The burning in my chest was unbearable, rising up my gullet before blasting out a breath of flames. It was difficult to swallow, I could hardly breathe. I screamed as another blast of pain ran through me. Gasping for air as if I'd come up after holding my breath for too long under water, heat flowed down my throat and through my body. *Was I on fire?*

I looked at my hands – no longer human, scaly and emerald with talons like shining swords. My senses enhanced, I could smell the earth, feel the trees outside calling for me to show myself. I felt strange. I hurtled out of the cave, my legs clumsy as I lurched myself into the sky. I rode the warm air currents, free as a bird. It was unexpectedly invigorating. I flew high above the island, glancing down at the land below me, a vision of wonder: Magae's beauty in all its splendour.

Filled with a perfect equanimity, a celebration of the elements within my soul, I could see for miles, other islands and infinite landscapes. I thought at that moment, I might live forever. I didn't want to ever shapeshift back. But the euphoria was short-lived as I detected an area of land, dry and spoiled, over-farmed and polluted; then another area the same. Another…animals lost, habitats ruined…and then another…and still more. My mood changed like a switch had been flicked. A surge of coldness took over my spirit, savage and brutal as I swooped back down in the direction of Sealgair. As I came into land, I opened my jaws to bare my teeth…and that's when it all went wrong.

8

OUR MISSION

I spat down a fiery rain onto the Isle of Sealgair, forcing my friends' animal totems to scatter aimlessly, not knowing where to run, as they searched desperately for cover. I landed on my muscular hind legs, causing the ground to shudder and crack beneath me. Fire continued to spread like gravy, bubbling over the ground. Screams and moans filled the air, echoing down to the coast. A deep-throated trumpet caught my attention. As the smoke cleared a little, there in front of me was the source of the sound, an elephant, shepherding the animals away amid falling debris and fiery chaos.

With a high-pitched howl, I took a swipe at the elephant with my talons, slashing its head, causing it to fall. As it staggered back up, blood trickling down its face, rage continued to course through my huge skeleton like poison, ready to release a deadly fury on anyone who got in my way, starting with the Dwellers at what they'd done to Magae. The elephant looked over its surroundings then, using its thick trunk, it sucked everything up. Before I had a chance to process what was going on, the elephant blasted the hot contents of its trunk up into my eyes with such a force I was temporarily blinded. Screaming out, I thrashed my heavy wings haphazardly, demolishing everything within my wingspan, filling the air with a cacophony of noise; clashing and cracking over terrified screams and cries. That's when I felt the blistering pain through my underbelly. The elephant had pierced me with one of its tusks. A feeling of torture so intense my legs gave way and I fell on my side with such a thud I think I saw the elephant leave the ground momentarily with a bounce.

"Ellery...find your meadow..."

The pain in my belly gripped me so tightly it was like having my innards squeezed. Each breath was agony.

"Ellery...slow down. Take a slow breath. Think of calm... Think of Lionel, Kessie, your mum on Giftmas morning. Dancing, singing...friendship, love and kindness...all the values you hold dear. The dragon is a protector, not a destroyer. We all get angry but you have to learn to use your anger with intelligence. You know that. Dave has told you so many times. Fighting rage with more rage gets you nowhere. If you have the ability to channel your anger with intelligence, then others will follow your lead. Kindness will always be stronger than hatred."

I closed my eyes and let the words wash over me as I strained every sinew to return to the meadow of sweet-smelling grass and honeysuckle. I grew cold and shivery.

"Open your eyes."

As I opened my eyes, which were stinging like mad, darkness had lifted and dawn was on its way. Myerscough was kneeling over me, dropping large blobs of blood onto my chest from a nasty gash on the side of his head. My heart pumped hard as I looked for my friends, fearing the worst. They were sitting by a smashed gravestone, covered in cuts and bruises. Many of the gravestones looked as though they'd been ripped from the earth. The church ruin was rubble, only small portions of stonework remained. The place looked like a war zone. Letty's face was dirty and streaked where she'd been crying. I think Kemp had been crying too.

"Can you sit up?" asked Myerscough.

I nodded, moving gingerly to an upright position. I looked down at my fleece, which was bloody round my middle.

"It's not as bad as it looks," said Myerscough. He took off his shirt and tore it into pieces, then wrapped it tightly around my wounded belly.

"You could have killed all your friends. What were you thinking? What were any of you thinking, trying this?"

"We thought—" I started, struggling to pronounce my words as my lips were sore and blistered. I suppose that's what happens when you breathe fire.

"Don't!" snapped Myerscough, his hand raised like a traffic policeman. "It was a rhetorical question. *You lot*," he yelled at my friends. "Follow me back to the medical building – then we'll talk. In fact, *I'll* talk, *you'll* listen."

He helped me to my feet but the pain in my stomach left me bent double and feeling faint. Before I knew it, Myerscough had scooped me up in his arms and set off back, with my friends trailing behind in silence.

I'm not sure how we reached the medical building or even how long it took. I was in and out of consciousness.

Myerscough laid me down on a bed while my friends hovered sheepishly nearby. The medical building must've been the old prison hospital. It needed a serious makeover. I reckon Florence Nightingale would have been at home in here. The room was grey and grim. Two lines of metal beds on wheels, and only one tiny window for just a peep of natural orange light as the sun rose outside. I'm sure the bed at the end had restraints attached, probably for restricting violent prisoners...or maybe it was for naughty school kids.

My heart sped up when Dr Ramsay scuttled over to me. She was our Chocomestry teacher, a doctor of *chocolate* – I'm not sure she even knew how to do proper medical stuff. I suppose Dr Wilberforce must still have been at Quinton House.

"It's going to need a couple of stitches, but you'll live, dear. I've seen worse," said Ramsay. "And that head needs looking at, Hendrick," she said, looking at Myerscough's bloody face.

Myerscough waved off her words like annoying flies and headed for the door where Mitchell and Guru Aabavaana stood. He probably didn't want Ramsay anywhere near his head in case she tried to stick it together with chocolate mousse.

"I'm sorry," I croaked to my friends, who were being tended to by a youngish man, a nurse perhaps, who cleaned and dressed their cuts. "I didn't know. I..." I trailed off, trying to catch my breath between sobs and jabs of pain. "I don't want the dragon totem. I've never wanted it. I just want to be normal. I never intended to hurt anyone."

Orford snarled. Nyle put his arm around me. "You weren't to know," he said kindly. "Not sure we should try that again, though."

"You didn't do much," said Thomas to Orford.

"Me? What the hell was I meant to do? She tried to kill us all."

Myerscough turned his head sharply from his conversation, just visible outside the door, silencing us instantly.

Dr Ramsay brought over a tray of six steaming hot chocolates with a sympathetic smile.

"Here," she said, passing them out. "This will make you feel better."

Slurping in silence, wincing as it stung my lips, I knew we were in too much trouble to think up an excuse that would be half believable.

Myerscough walked back into the room, heading for the large cabinet in the corner, followed by the other two teachers. He pulled out a bottle of something and a glass, then poured himself a stiff drink which he slugged down before pouring another. He then allowed Mitchell to stitch up his head.

"You're lucky," said Aab, looking at my wound.

I didn't feel lucky, not even a little bit. It looked better than it felt, which didn't make sense. I'd been skewered on an elephant's tusk, after all.

"Okay, boys and girls," began Myerscough, clearing his throat as he strode towards us. "What have you learned from this?"

"Orford's definitely not a dragon guide," said Nyle.

"What's that supposed to mean?" snapped Orford, his nostrils flaring.

"You were useless. You didn't do *anything*."

"What the hell was I meant to do? We didn't stand a chance against *that* monster." He pointed at me with an angry finger before nursing a couple of nasty grazes on his elbows. No wonder he was in such a bad mood.

I pushed my hair behind my ear, feeling awkward and guilty, not to mention hundreds of other negative feelings which I knew I shouldn't begin to visit.

Aab put his hands together in namaste and looked at me. I nodded and mimicked.

"Okay," said Aab. "Perhaps that was the wrong line of questioning." He laughed. "This is not about blaming. This is about learning. Firstly, and most importantly, we all know that Nash is still around, I'm afraid, and hell-bent on ridding Magae of Dwellers. Your negative energy," he continued, looking at me, "will draw his attention, like a magnet attracted to an opposite pole. He will feel your negativity and head for it, knowing that when you react in this way, although you feel strong, you are actually at your most vulnerable. It is at this time that he will be able to grab those gifts of yours and use them unwisely. If he takes your life force from you, you will perish, Ellery…and countless others too, I dare say."

I swallowed hard.

"Your dragon totem is a gift from Magae, and as such is powerful – too powerful, perhaps – certainly at this moment in time. This is why you need help from your teachers to keep it under control."

I looked across to Myerscough. "You tried to kill me, *Dad*."

"Ha! Do you really think it's that easy to kill a dragon? I wasn't even close, my girl."

"How *do* you kill a dragon, then, sir?" asked Thomas as though he'd need to use this knowledge in the future.

"You either cut its head off..." answered Myerscough, prompting me to subconsciously reach for my neck with both shaking hands.

"Or stab it in the heart...which was a long way from where I grazed you."

"*Grazed me?*" I begged to differ. "You *impaled* me."

"Anyway," continued Aab before I had a chance to challenge my father further. "You've got to learn to control it...train it, if you like. This is Magae's totem and you are an extension of her. This is why you were so angry. Whatever happens to the earth is happening emotionally to you too. You've got to master calmness and kindness within yourself and it will project to everyone around you. You are the master of your own fate. You might not be able to control what goes on outside you, but you can control what goes on inside you. Do you understand, Ellery?"

"Yes, sir." I nodded.

"In rage, you join forces with Nash; with a cool head you can become one with the entire cosmos. You need to take responsibility for your gift, Ellery, before your future deserts you. We will help you. All of us, not just your teachers, but your friends as well."

"Does this mean Orford's not her guide, then? I mean, a lizard and a bat don't make a dragon after all, do they?" stated Nyle, with a slightly smug look on his face.

"Make a dragon?" repeated Mitchell, followed by a hearty laugh. "That's very clever of you but I don't think it works like that." He took a swig of whatever Myerscough had drunk, then licked his lips contentedly. "Bats have a way of making one focus beyond the norm. They see through dark areas that others do not, so combined with a lizard they would connect with mythical creatures, offering skills to adapt to new situations. An invaluable guide, I'd say, to make sure your heart is in control rather than your ego. But we are all here to guide her with our spirit assets. This, unfortunately, is what many of Nash's contemporaries failed to acknowledge."

"What do you mean, sir?" asked Orford.

"We all regret not helping Nash. We all should have done more to persuade him to call upon a guru and not a Magaecian master to calm him, but so many were too afraid."

"Well, I don't blame them," said Orford, folding his arms across his chest. "You can count me out."

I sympathised with him. I must've been terrifying as a dragon. No one in their right mind would sign up for this job.

"Typical," muttered Nyle under his breath.

"He'll come around," whispered Letty. "So what can we do to help her, sir?"

"That's easy," Myerscough replied. "You've got to do something positive."

Aab nodded in agreement.

"Life is under threat – not just for Magaecians or Dwellers but all life," Myerscough continued.

"That's negative," I said, sarcastically.

"Yes, it is, but if you'll let me continue without rudely butting in, it's a problem that humans have created so we, as humans, are in command of what happens next. If you hope someone else will sort it out for you, then things will never change. All of us must make a change – a positive change, rather than dwelling on what is negative. You, in particular, Ellery, must find the positive in this situation."

"But why is it all up to me to change the world?" I said. "I mean, just because I'm an ebonoid, it doesn't automatically mean I can magically put everything right."

"Haha!" blasted Myerscough. "You're fourteen, Ellery. You can't change the world alone, but together we can make a world of change." He stopped for a minute. "I'm not sure that makes any sense. This stuff's stronger than it looks," he said, eyeing his empty glass.

"The thing is, Ellery," added Mitchell, "by doing something positive for Magae, you will calm your totem. By calming your totem, you will be nearer to becoming one with her. Try spending more time surrounded by nature. Disconnect from modern technology for a bit so that you can establish a bond with her. This will help you and your dragon connect. Work outside more to feel and enjoy Magae's elements – the wind, the sun and the rain on your skin."

Mitchell looked across at the other two teachers, probably hoping for them to back him up with more suggestions. After a couple of silent stares, Myerscough cleared his throat again and began his slightly slurred address.

"You must do your bit for Magae. As an ebonoid, by helping her, you will subsequently help yourself. It's not something you can undertake alone, of course, but with the right spells you'll unite others to see we have humanity in common. Remember always that Magae will recover, whatever we dreadful humans choose to do. It's the humans that might not make it if we choose unwisely. It's not going to be easy to reclaim what is lost; to regenerate trees and forests; but we can encourage respect for Magae and change destructive habits in favour of preserving our environment for generations to come. The trick is to inspire, rather than dictate. If we stop dwelling on the past and accept the present, then we'll have hope for the future." Myerscough paused again, losing his train of thought in the middle of his speech. "I'm not sure that makes sense either, does it?"

"Our wants outstrip what Magae can supply," continued Aab, attempting to help Myerscough out. "We need to cut down so that those with too much can help those with not enough. We have to educate. Get Dweller kids your age to touch the soil, feel the insects, grow some food. Don't focus on what isn't working but on what is and can, to heal Magae so that we may all benefit from it."

"We can get rid of all the plastic bottles and stuff around here. They're everywhere. I noticed them as soon as we got off the ferry," said Thomas, which got a bit of a moan from Orford.

"Good start," said Myerscough. "No one said it would be easy, but if you wait for something to happen, nothing will. You've got to go out there and make a difference, kids." He paused. "Right…I think that's enough for one night. You'll all get a yellow for leaving the building after hours, of course. Consider yourselves lucky to get off so lightly but let me warn you – next time, should there be one, there will be nothing but the severest of consequences. Do you understand?"

"Yes, sir," we chorused like a group of robots.

"Now, go back to your rooms before I change my mind and don't leave your beds until it's time for breakfast. Go!"

As my friends scurried out of the room, Myerscough sat on the end of my bed. A heavy expression marred his face as he rubbed his stubbly chin.

"Are you really all right, Ellery?"

I shook my head, catching tears with my tongue to stop them stinging my sore lips.

"I'm frightened. What if I become like Nash?"

"You won't," replied Myerscough with a gentle smile.

"I think I already have."

"What do you mean?"

"I know what Nash feels – the rage at the damage Dwellers have done to Magae. They've completely overrun the planet and wrecked it. I don't think I'm going to be able to control the hate running through me. It's so overwhelming. I know I shouldn't but I think I might even agree with Nash. Mitchell was right – it *is* inevitable, I *am* going to become like him."

"No, you're not. There's a difference between you and Nash. You are part Dweller and were brought up as such. You see the world from both sides – like your uncle did. You've experienced a change in your outlook in just the short time you've been with Magaecians. This is what makes you so special. You know that Dwellers can change. This gives us hope. Magaecians and Dwellers are the same species; Magae can't split them into those that care and those that don't.

That's why it's up to us to change everyone's point of view so that future generations get the future they deserve. Killing to survive has never been a Magaecian option. You know that."

He took my hands, swallowing them up in his enormous fists.

"Meet me here after school tomorrow. We can make a start on that elemental energy of yours," he said softly.

"Okay, Hendrick, she needs to get some sleep now. Say your goodnights, please," said Dr Ramsay, ushering Myerscough out of the room after he kissed me on the head. "And Ellery will, under no circumstances, be attending classes tomorrow. She needs to rest for a couple of days, at least."

I closed my eyes, feeling less than enthusiastic about honing my pyrotechnic skills with Myerscough. However, my initial anguish at being left in the care of a *pretend* doctor was now reduced. At least she'd got me out of school for a couple of days.

9

THE RACE

My friends got one day off; I got two. It wasn't nearly enough, but I reckon it was Myerscough's way of putting us off for any future ideas of rule-breaking. Despite feeling dreadful, my stitches – *real* stitches, not chocolate ones – were smarting across my stomach, I was surprised to find that the day flew by. I hadn't slept properly since the dreaded dragon event, so I wasn't holding out much hope of keeping awake through even one lesson, but foraging spells with Lameko was actually really good fun. We found an abundance of fruits and nuts in the forest behind the old prison, which we were allowed to sample. The beechnuts were delicious to nibble once you'd scraped off the outer skin. Lameko warned us not to eat too many though, as we'd end up with the runs! Letty didn't pick that much, too busy sketching new plants and berries. There was a huge harvest of raspberries and elderberries so we were able to fill our bags, ready to enjoy spells to make jams, syrup and wine – although the wine spell was only for Year 12s. Lameko told us the Latin names for all the stuff but I couldn't remember any of them except the words for raspberry, *Rubus idaeus*, and that was only because it sounded a bit like "rubbish idiot".

After lunch we spent the afternoon studying cleaning spells with Mrs Chaudhry, a short woman who barely reached my shoulders. From behind she looked like a kid from primary school. It was basically a chemistry lesson on how to make your own washing-up liquid and surface cleaner. Thomas put too much vinegar in his so it smelled like the local chippy.

I left my friends at four o'clock with a heavy heart to meet up with Myerscough outside the medical building. I walked past a group of Year 12s in the middle of a lesson with Mr Rivers on "how to get to know a tree". Myerscough taught me that every tree had something unique about it. They were like people with distinguishing characteristics. During the summer, we found a tree behind the pub in Tribourne with a huge hollow, big enough to climb inside so that you could see the tiny cracks where insects hid. He said there was nothing more naturally fashionable than a tree. Lively, undimmed and exuberant in the spring, thickly styled green tiers for summer, the boldest statement of red and orange flares for autumn and the most modest of minimal browns in winter.

As I approached the medical building, Myerscough was already there. He signalled with a pointed finger towards the herb garden.

"Follow me," he shouted.

We sat together on an old wooden bench, weathered by the seasons. The scent of rosemary, thyme and sage tickled at my nostrils, sweet and pungent.

"As an ebonoid with a dragon totem, Ellery, you have an untapped energy that could make you a master of the elements. This doesn't mean I have to go out and buy you a superhero cape and matching tights, or negotiate your own chat show; it means you must exercise control if you're to be of any benefit to Magae. It's easy to get too big for your boots and it's easy to underestimate how quickly you can lose control, which is why you need supervision if you're to visit your totem. As you master the elements, so the dragon's power will become more controllable. Be patient. That's all I ask. Right – let's make a start, shall we?" he said, as if he were going to teach me a magic trick.

"What were you thinking about when the fire started in Dormly station; when you nearly fell to your death in the Quinton House tunnel; when the shots were fired at Oracle Farm?"

"I dunno," I said. "Probably of being anywhere but where I actually was."

"Where?"

"Back home with Mum." I paused. "A-a-and you, of course," I added, hoping it didn't sound too insincere, although I know it did.

Myerscough grunted. "Were there any smells, any feelings that might have overwhelmed you or produced a funny sensation – pins and needles, perhaps?"

"My tongue went all tingly," I offered. "Mint was the smell that reminded me of home – Mum's mint tea and

Lionel's nose from rummaging through the mint bush. Mum's fresh bread as well…"

Myerscough nodded. "Okay. I need you to stand up with me."

I did as he asked.

"Now look at the bench in front of you and think of all the things you just mentioned that made you feel at home, safe, secure." He walked off, bent down to pick some leaves, then passed them to me. They were mint leaves. I suppose that's why he wanted to meet in the herb garden; he knew there would be something in here that would remind me of the smell of home. It was a cunning move – a bit sneaky, in my opinion.

"Smell the mint, use your thoughts, then think of the air element and lift the bench."

"What?"

"You heard me. Smell the mint, use your thoughts, then lift the bench," he repeated.

I took a deep breath and followed his instructions… nothing. I shook my head. "It's not working."

"You're going to have to try longer than three seconds, Ellery." Myerscough laughed.

Ten minutes went by…another ten…nothing. Another… still nothing. I don't know how long we carried on for, but nothing happened.

"Hmmm. Directing an energy takes time and practice. We'll try this again at the end of the week. Until then, practise, practise, practise. Always positive, never negative." He smiled, something he didn't do much, then waved across the garden to Mitchell who was waiting for him and headed in that direction, leaving me standing there like a bit of a twit.

✳✳✳

Term whizzed by and Giftmas was fast approaching, but my *gifts* had yet to surface. I'd spent all term practising, missing Mitchell's totem classes to practise empowering the elements but I hadn't got a lot better. If I'm honest, I hadn't got *any* better. I raided the beach for a new totem stone, a lovely smooth pebble, tinged with green and brown, which I decoupaged with a dragon. Myerscough thought it best not to use it until I'd worked on my temper, redirecting any anger and negative ebonoid energy into a positive force. Only then would I be more successful on calling on Magae's elements. It didn't work. I tried not to let it get to me even though Nyle kept teasing me about it. Instead, I made a decision to focus my energies on something else, something worthwhile, something positive to calm my totem. My friends and I set up a group called *H.A.M.S.*, which stood for the *Healthy Appreciation of Magae Society*. It was growing in numbers every week as we combined with kids in the village. We passed on our ideas of how to lower carbon footprints in Dweller schools – like using less plastic, providing school lunches with less meat, wasting less. We also got the kitchen staff at Manburgh to open up our vegetable and herb gardens to the rest of the island so that we shared our produce with everyone. It was very popular except among those who thought the prison was haunted. They didn't come anywhere near it. Letty wrote to a number of Scottish and English

MPs about planting fruit trees in urban areas. The idea was to allow anyone, particularly those struggling financially, to pick fruit, free of charge. Some MPs didn't reply, some didn't want to know but many agreed to help. We were all doing our bit for Magae and it felt incredible. In fact, I'm not sure I'd ever felt so fulfilled or so happy. Helping others really wasn't that difficult and yet the rewards were enormous, far greater than any of us could ever have expected. As we engaged more people, casting our spells, so they engaged with others, passing on a love for their environment; more were respecting Magae's reserves; strangers were coming together in a common bond to do more for their planet. We still had a long way to go, of course, but it was working.

It was the last week of term and the village was holding a *pick-up-the-most-plastic* race along the beach. It was a timed event – fifteen minutes to pick up as much plastic littered on the shore line as possible. The team collecting the most would be declared the winner and would get to ignite the enormous Christmas pudding made by Chef MacBrennan. She'd arrived the day before in readiness to spend Giftmas in Sealgair with her husband. She seemed to visit our year group more than the others in the school. I think she had a soft spot for us. Letty thought she just fancied Mr Mitchell. Mind you, Letty thought everyone fancied Mr Mitchell. A collection of pubs and fish and chip shops along the seafront were probably the main contributors to the event from their tossed-out polystyrene boxes and water bottles, together with crisp and pork scratching packets. Year 9s took the steep path down to the shore while Year 12s used the cable cars. Villagers gathered, donning woolly hats and scarves, waving flags and banners in the icy wind. School kids grouped into teams, teeth chattering as they whispered tactics before the race began. The rules were: no collecting sharp objects or anything vaguely contaminated with dubious droppings, which I think meant nothing covered in dog poo! Other than that, it was *anything goes*. We mixed up our teams to have Dweller kids among Magaecian kids, taking coloured bibs to differentiate our groups. Letty made a beeline for Ashkii Mitchell's Green team, putting Kemp's nose out of joint. He joined me and Thomas in the Yellow team, while Nyle and Orford grouped with the Blues. Each team was given a huge hessian sack, then taken to different areas of the beach to await the signal to start. Radella Tewksbury from Year 12 held our sack in one hand, using the other to signal a thumbs up to the referee that we were ready. A loud blast, like a ship's foghorn – and we were off.

I was happy to be doing something positive, something that would make a difference. It was so easy and such fun as we scavenged away to retrieve as much as possible, chucking the plastic haphazardly into the sack.

"Don't forget there's a prize for the most unusual find on the beach," said Radella.

"I think I might win that," squealed Thomas, waving an old canister of Scandinavian bug spray in the air.

I found a headless Barbie doll and a juice box dating back to 1989. Kemp was still in a huff with Letty until I suggested we try to beat Ashkii's team. He seemed to pick up steam after that and found an empty box of Tic Tacs with the price 1p on it, so it must've been really old. The wind was biting, my fingers lost all sensation and yet, I didn't feel cold. As the foghorn blasted out again to signal the end of the race, the beach looked amazing. Clear and sparkly as its icy surface glistened in the sun.

The large bags were brought to the referee's tent which was actually just a small put-you-up gazebo, unlikely to remain upright for much longer in the wind. The collected plastic was to be taken to Mr MacDougall's workshop where it would be converted into ecobrick stools to sell at the Sealgair fair at the village hall on Christmas Eve. We were all invited. They were offering mince pies and mulled wine.

As I sat chatting with Letty to see if she'd got anywhere with Ash – which she hadn't – a chilling scream tore through the air. In the distance, Orford was sandwiched between two large men dressed in black overcoats and scarves. Nash must have sent them. They forced Orford off his feet and dragged him away. He kicked out and tossed his head about, smashing one of them in the face, resulting in the man letting go. It wasn't long before the man rose back up to knee poor Orford in the back, sending him straight to the ground.

I sprang from the spot to get to him. As I raced to get nearer, Orford turned his head back and screamed out, "Nyle!"

I looked back but Nyle wasn't there.

"Nyle!" he screamed out again before the same man that kneed him jabbed him hard in the ribs.

I thought my heart might run out of beats it was going so fast. Closing my eyes for a moment to compose myself, I knew that using my negative energy could stop those men but it could also hurt Orford. I let go of my thoughts, my senses, and let Magae fill me with all her force. My hands trembled as I tried to work out how I'd saved Orford at the farm, how I'd escaped with Nyle from the Quinton House tunnel. I think it might have been sheer panic, as there was no other explanation. Not really something I could produce on tap. Maybe that's why I hadn't been getting anywhere with Myerscough. Sheer panic was probably an understatement as my tongue tingled and the sand beneath my feet rumbled like a river of energy. As my friend struggled, violently dragged away by Nash's two thugs, I extended my arms, palms out. I somehow pushed the air so that it stirred up the sand – a whirling vortex growing bigger and stronger, heading straight for them, viciously colliding with them like a bowling ball striking all three, splaying them out flat. The two men rose to their feet like a couple of drunks and made an unsteady run for it, leaving Orford stretched out like a corpse. As they headed away, I pushed the air again to swirl it into a high wall of sand, solidified by ocean spray, which both men unavoidably slammed into. Out cold.

Oblivious to what was going on around me, teachers and villagers had shot down the beach to help Orford. Mitchell and Lameko grabbed the men, forcefully marching them up to the gazebo, slapping them about here and there as they did so.

Myerscough tapped me on the shoulder and whispered, "Good girl. I knew you could do it."

As Orford was tended to by the dreaded Dr Ramsay, no doubt offering him a chocolate transfusion or maybe a high dose of chocolate fudge brownie, I looked about for Nyle to gloat about my elemental powers finally emerging to save the day, but I couldn't find him.

"Nyle!" I called out.

No reply.

"Nyle!" I called again but he was nowhere.

"They've taken him," cried Orford. "It was a trap," he continued, hiding his face in his sandy hands.

"What do you mean?" I asked, pushing in front of Dr Ramsay.

"It was a trap."

"I don't understand."

"Everyone was so busy saving me, they didn't notice Nyle being snatched out of view."

"What?" My heart hammered so hard against my ribs I wondered if anyone else could hear it. "Why would anyone take Nyle?" I demanded.

"Because Nash knows how close a friend he is to you," spluttered Orford, wiping his nose with the back of his hand, spreading wet sand all over his face.

"How could he possibly know that?"

Orford didn't answer. He covered his mouth with his hand, blinking tears onto the sand and shaking his head. "I think it might be my fault."

"You told him?" I yelled.

"No. Not exactly…"

"How could you?"

"Please, Ellery…just listen to me…"

"Don't talk to me!" I screamed. "I knew I shouldn't have trusted you. I knew it."

Orford gripped his chest as I continued my rant. I shouldn't have persisted in such a rage – I knew I'd hurt him, but I couldn't help it.

"He's your cousin – he's family. Nash will kill him. I'll never forgive you. *Never*. I hate you!"

Blood oozed from Orford's nose.

10

THINKING LIKE NASH

Myerscough grabbed the back of my hoodie and hoisted me up into the air and away from Orford.

"Stop!" he blasted, throwing me onto a beach chair, away from everybody else on the beach. "Don't you understand, this is what Nash wants? He needs your anger. It's the only way he can latch onto your life force and the only way he can take another shot at your dragon and everything that comes with it. You are playing straight into his hands. He's messing with your head and you can't allow him to."

"I don't care," I yelled back. "He's got my friend. He's got Nyle…" I broke down, sobbing, slipping off the chair to crumple onto my knees. "We've got to get him back."

"Yes, we must," said Myerscough, pulling me to his chest as he sat down beside me on the sand. "But first you've got to stop jumping to the wrong conclusions all the time. Your friend, Orford…"

"He's not my friend," I spat.

"He *is* your friend. He didn't tell Nash you were close to Nyle. It was Orford's mother, Kimberley Nibley-Soames. Besides, it's probably something Nash already knew. He must have threatened her. Perhaps he said he'd hurt Orford if she didn't give him the names of your closest friends."

"So! Orford still snitched."

"No, he didn't. When Orford's mum asked him for the names, Orford refused to tell her."

"You're just making it up now. How can you possibly know all this?"

"I know because Orford's mum met with Dave, and Dave told me of her meeting."

I felt my face heat up knowing Dave must've told Myerscough of *my* meeting too, with Nyle. The woman's voice I should have recognised that night, I think it might have belonged to Orford's mum.

"Dave said how frightened Kimberley was, expecting Nash to return with more power than ever before to kill us all. She asked Dave for guidance but Dave reckoned it was more of a repentance. She was desperate to seek forgiveness for what she'd done. She didn't say what she'd done, of course, but she must have already gone to Nash with Nyle's name because that was the one name she already knew."

Maybe I *had* jumped to the wrong conclusion. Orford's mum must have come to school on the first day to get the names from him.

"Kimberley Nibley-Soames feared for Orford's life, so she must've given Nash Nyle's name in return for Orford's safety. She shouldn't have done it but she was trying to protect her son like any mother might do."

"He screamed out Nyle's name," I said. "On the beach when they attacked him."

Myerscough nodded. "He must've seen it happening but was unable to help as Nash's men held Orford down."

"So, if his mum made this deal not to harm Orford, why did they try to kill him at the farm?"

"I don't think their intention was to kill him. I think their instructions were most likely to capture and torture him for names. Nyle Pinkerton wasn't a name Nash didn't already know, especially after he helped you last year. And I think we all know how good Nash is with fairness and keeping his word."

"But they were shooting at us."

"Yes. I reckon they lost more than their jobs for doing that. Nash won't want anyone to kill you before he has a shot at that dragon and your elemental energy."

"I think I owe Orford an apology," I said, looking down at my feet. I felt terrible. Why hadn't I given Orford the benefit of the doubt? I couldn't be a more dreadful friend. I was the opposite to *totally Hawk*, more like *totally Orc*, like one of those ugly, disgusting, evil goblin-monsters in *The Lord of the Rings*. I wondered if he'd even want to forgive me.

"Come on," said Myerscough, interrupting my thoughts. "We'll get the cable car up. You can apologise back at *The Palace*."

By the time we reached *The Palace* it was snowing. The warmth I'd felt on the beach had long since gone, turning into an icy depression. Staff ran around mindlessly, directing policemen all over the estate to look for Nyle.

I headed for the medical building to find Orford. His face was swollen and bruised and he was still crying. As he saw me approach, he grabbed his chest and neck in readiness for more ebonoid pain.

"I'm sorry," I said, running up to his bed to hug him.

He grunted as he moved away.

"I shouldn't have said all those things. If I could take them back, I would."

"Once you cast a spell, you can't retract it," said Orford.

"I know and I'm sorry. Will you ever forgive me?"

"I'll have to think about it."

I suppose I deserved that.

"I'm kidding." He laughed. "I know how it must've looked. I should have told you what my stupid mother might do."

"Don't say that. She did what any mother might do. She protected her son in the only way she saw possible."

"The *wrong* way."

"Maybe…but I still don't understand why Nash needs to know who my best friends are."

Orford glared at me. "I thought you were meant to be smart," he said. "I'm joking," he added quickly, obviously not wanting to test my temper again. "He needs to take the people you love to get the reaction you produced on the beach. That uncontrollable temper will be his ticket to your power, don't you see? You won't be able to control your anger if he hurts one of your friends, will you?"

I began chewing at one of my fingernails. He was right.

"It didn't occur to me before," continued Orford, "but I think I know what he might do next."

"What do you mean?"

"I mean, you've got to think like Nash. If it were me and I wanted to make you angry, I'd probably take each of your friends, one by one."

"What? *Why?*"

Orford gripped his chest, staring at me with a sarcastic smile and accompanying grimace. "Isn't it obvious?"

"Sorry." I put my hands together in namaste.

"You need to control your temper, Ellery, otherwise you're gonna make it too easy for him and he'll take your dragon."

"What are we going to do? I can't help being angry."

"That's where you're wrong," said Orford, with a smile and a pointed finger. "You *can* control your anger – I've seen you do it, Ellery. I'm just not sure Nash can control his and he's got so bloody much of it."

There was an awkward moment of silence before we both broke into a laugh. I pulled my dragon totem stone from my sandy pocket and handed it to him.

"What's this for?" he said.

"I think it might be safer with you. I'm a long way from calling it so you can keep it until I'm ready."

"Is this your way of saying that you trust me?"

"Maybe."

***

Magaecian Giftmas and Dweller Christmas came and went in a blur. Nothing was much fun knowing that Nyle might be undergoing torture sessions with Saxon Nash. Myerscough kept disappearing off with search parties but they always came back empty-handed. I still hung out with my friends even though Myerscough told me not to. He said I was putting them in unnecessary danger. I reckon he'd have locked me in my bedroom for the entire holiday if he thought he could've got away with it.

We started our second term on the Isle of Sealgair, which was so cold and bleak it made our school building look far more prison-like. Letty thought she heard screams one night from a ghost, although she admitted it might've been her mind playing tricks as it was just after she'd watched a scary film in the common room.

We slurped our hot chocolates during morning break, after a double period of survival spells with Mr Stone. The Year 12s said he was *Stone by name, stone by nature.* He was a tallish, average-build man, clean-shaven with short, dark hair but he was void of expression. His lesson followed the syllabus laid down by the B.E.E.F. (the British Environmental Education Federation), something he repeated over and over laboriously as he droned on and on like a bad politician. Letty took her sketch pad out after the first ten minutes, sketching a stone with Mr Stone's features on it.

Chatting together, Letty showed me another sketch she'd done. It was of Ashkii Mitchell.

"That's a really good likeness," I said.

"He doesn't know I even exist," she replied, drawing a large cross right the way through his face.

"What did you do that for?"

"I'm giving up on men. I don't understand how it works. I mean, I look much older than my age and I know I'm not bad-looking – better-looking than that Radella Tewksbury he seems to hang around with, anyway. I even puffed out my chest and put socks down my bra to make my boobs look bigger. If that didn't work, nothing will. I'm going to end up a nun."

"What?" I said, giggling. "It's got nothing to do with your boobs. He's not interested because he's probably not interested."

"That makes no sense at all."

"What I mean is that apart from the way he looks, which I admit is pleasing on the eye, you two have practically nothing in common. You love art, he loves cars."

"But he's so strong and brave. Kemp's so nervous all the time."

"Kemp seems nervous, but I'd say it's more cautious. You're friends with him because he's a hundred times braver than Ashkii Mitchell."

"What do you mean?"

"Kemp saved my life and probably all our lives last year. He allowed Nash's snake to swallow him up, knowing full well that it would most likely kill him. He risked everything for all of us. That's not something you find in many people you meet. Perhaps you're looking in the wrong place."

She didn't answer but I could tell my spell had had an effect.

We arranged to meet in the herb garden after school to discuss our ideas about how we might somehow calm Nash's temper and get Nyle back. I arrived first, followed by Thomas, Orford, then Kemp. Letty was late. I wondered why she was taking so long. I looked at my watch. She should have been here by now. I caught a glance of a small object under the bench. My heart came to an abrupt halt with a sense of dread before starting back up with the speed of a train. I bent down to pick up the object. Letty's sketch pad.

"No! Letty's been taken," cried Kemp, panic flooding his face and tears welling up in his eyes.

I opened the pad to her last sketch. It was a large worm.

11

GHOSTS AND KIDS

"**I**t's the worm I saw at Quinton House," I said, passing round the sketch, hoping Kemp didn't flick to the previous page to see the portrait of Ashkii.

"That's not any worm," said Orford. "That's a mythical worm, you know? W...Y...R...M. It's an armless, legless serpent-dragon with poisonous breath. It looks harmless enough until it quadruples in size."

"That's not good," said Thomas.

"No, not good at all," reiterated Orford.

"But if Nash already has a dragon, then why would he need Ellery's?" asked Thomas.

"Because Ellery's dragon is related to Magae and as such, reacts with her elements. Nash's dragon, if you can call it that, is just an extension of his alter ego."

"What does that even mean?" asked Thomas, scrunching up his nose as if he'd smelled something horrible.

"It means we've got trouble," I said.

"Help!" yelled Thomas in a high-pitched voice. *"HELP!"* he screamed again, spitting out saliva as the pitch dropped an octave lower.

"What are you doing?" snapped Orford. "All the teachers are running this way, now."

"We need to tell them Letty's gone," answered Thomas defiantly. "We've got to tell the teachers."

It was odd to hear that statement coming from Thomas, it was usually Kemp wanting to stick to all the rules but he gave no response.

"What's going on?" bellowed out Myerscough before he'd even reached us. Mitchell and Lameko were right behind him with Dr Ramsay lagging quite a long way behind them.

"Letty's missing," announced Thomas, hands on hips, which seemed to be a regular stance for him lately.

Myerscough's forehead creased with concern as Thomas passed him the wyrm sketch. His concern seemed to grow as he rubbed his chin, then he cleared his throat to speak to the other teachers.

"We need to get a group together before the last ferry goes for the night."

"That doesn't leave us very long, Hendrick," said Mitchell, looking at his watch.

"I know. We must hurry." He turned to me and my friends, a grave expression marring his face. "Go back inside and stay there. Don't get any wise ideas to look for your friends yourselves. Do you understand me? *Do you?*"

"Yes, sir," we chorused.

He dashed off with the teachers, Dr Ramsay struggling to keep up again.

"Don't look for your friends yourselves," I repeated sarcastically. "Why not? The teachers aren't getting anywhere."

"I agree. We can't wait for the adults to find Letty and Nyle," said Kemp, rocking back and forth. "We've got to do something."

"But Myerscough said—" started Thomas.

"We need a plan," I interrupted.

All heads nodded. It didn't take much to convince Thomas, who was always up for adventure, although I had a horrible feeling our so-called plan could turn into a suicide mission.

"Nash needs you alive," said Orford, stroking his chin as if he had stubble, which he didn't. "If he kills you then he can't take back the dragon."

"Perhaps he's hiding them on the island," suggested Kemp, indifferent to Orford's suggestions, obviously wanting to start searching for Letty straight away.

"All the teachers have searched the island several times. Even the villagers have looked," I replied.

"Mind you," began Orford. "Maybe it's too obvious."

"What do you mean?" I asked impatiently. Orford seemed to be working the answers out in his head and not sharing them.

"Nash has to be on the island to do his kidnapping, right? To take a hostage to the mainland, you need a ferry and if he's taking ferries with abducted kids, someone would see him. They must. Myerscough's got eyes everywhere. He knows practically everybody on the island especially at the port. He couldn't get away with it, not without Myerscough knowing."

We all stared at Orford, shrugging, none the wiser.

"Come on," he continued. "He hasn't been spotted because…"

"Because he's got a good disguise?" offered Thomas.

"He hasn't been spotted because he's never left the island," said Orford, shaking his head at Thomas.

"I don't understand," said Thomas with his hands-on-hip stance again.

"Why hasn't anyone found him, then?" asked Kemp.

"Where would you go if you wanted to hide, if you didn't want to be found by Nash?"

"Somewhere his ebonoid energy wouldn't work," said Kemp.

"Somewhere Myerscough would be," I added.

"Exactly," said Orford.

"I don't understand," I replied.

"He wants Myerscough to believe Nyle and now Letty are off the island so that he leaves the island to go search for them."

"And that leaves us all without Myerscough's shielding immunity," I added.

"Where's Myerscough now?" asked Thomas, twitching. His eyes widened to look a bit manic.

"He was going to take the last ferry off the island," I replied.

"Exactly," said Orford, raising his eyebrows.

"But I still don't understand," said Thomas. "I thought everyone checked the island."

"They did," said Orford. "But maybe he's hidden them in plain sight. Maybe we've overlooked somewhere so completely obvious that we've missed it right in front of our eyes."

"Like where?" demanded Thomas.

"The mountain?" said Kemp. "Mount Ghuthan isn't just occupied by *The Palace*. There are areas for birdwatching, refuges for hikers and bikers."

"Nah," said Orford. "You're overthinking this. When everyone thought Nash must've taken Nyle off the island, they switched their search to Aberdeen, London, Tribourne…all over the place. In other words, they stopped looking on the Isle of Sealgair."

"But there's nowhere left," said Thomas.

"Oh yes there is," said Orford, raising his eyebrows again.

I knew what he was thinking and so did Kemp.

"Please don't say you think we should look there," said Kemp with a shudder.

Orford nodded.

"Where?" asked Thomas. "Where shouldn't you say?"

Kemp swallowed so hard I heard the gulp travel from his throat down his windpipe. His eyes bulged against his now whiter than white complexion.

"The old Manburgh Prison cells," whispered Kemp, as if saying it out loud might call upon the Devil.

"Not the haunted ones?" blurted out Thomas.

"Yes," said Orford. "Let's meet up tonight."

"In the dark?"

"Most nights are usually dark, Thomas," said Orford with a dismissive wave of his hand.

Most nights are usually dark, but this night was particularly so. We all had torches on our phones but there was never much of a signal on Mount Ghuthan, so if we did need help, we'd have to scream for it. It was freezing, an aching cold that nagged at your bones. I pulled my scarf over my mouth to warm my face but it only accentuated my overly fast breathing as my heart pumped too quickly. The old prison cells were the other side of the cemetery. Standing in the grounds of the church and abbey ruins, such a mess after my disastrous dragon episode, a discouraging sensation passed through me.

"You okay?" asked Orford.

"Fine," I replied, despite the fact that the hairs on the back of my neck prickled as I watched the night shadows shifting back and forth.

Thomas's body jerked with every snap of a twig.

"Come on, it's this way," said Orford.

The prison cells loomed in sight; grotesque metal grilles barred the few windows that perforated the crumbling stone block.

"Are you sure about this?" asked Thomas.

"Yes," snapped Kemp, which was the first word he'd spoken since we'd set off.

"It feels evil to me," continued Thomas. "There might be prisoners' tormented spirits in there."

"Shhhh," hissed Orford.

Thomas had a point. Not that there might be evil spirits but more that there was a strange energy that I couldn't define. I didn't know if anyone else felt it, so I decided to keep it to myself.

The building was wrapped in overgrown weeds and ivy as if Magae had reclaimed it for herself. The walls were dimpled and decayed, huge chunks gnawed away with time. The entrance door hung open, askew on its hinges like a mouth gaping wide to devour us. We crept through, Orford first, then me, Thomas and lastly, Kemp. A painful knot in my stomach was urging me to turn back. I couldn't shake the disturbing feeling that we were not alone.

It was so dark inside, and a strong musty smell hit me as soon as I took my first step. The bitter wind tore through the front door, whistling eerily through the building. As my eyes adjusted, I could pick out the shape of the prison cells. We tiptoed past each one, pushing the heavy metal doors open to reveal empty box-like rooms, depressing, bare and nasty. After the last cell was a long corridor, shrouded in blackness. As we trod carefully through it, hardly daring to breathe, I could just about make out a flight of spiral stairs in front of Orford. Thomas suddenly shrieked, flailing his hands about in front of him as he'd got tangled in a curtain of cobwebs.

"You're fine," I whispered, wiping them off him.

An icy chill crawled up my back. I didn't believe in ghosts but that weird energy was giving me jitters. My hands trembled so much it was difficult to keep hold of my phone. The moaning wind seemed to follow us, echoing through the building, rattling the door hinges.

"I can hear footsteps," whispered Kemp.

"I-i-is that a g-ghost?" stuttered Thomas.

"Of course not," said Orford, far too snappily.

My heart lurched. Someone else was definitely in the building. I could hear a faint cry.

Thomas swallowed hard. "Should we turn back and get help?"

"I think it might be too late for that now, Thomas. What if it's Nyle or Letty?" I said.

"We need to stick together," whispered Orford. "Turn off your phones. It might be safer."

At the top of the stairwell was another flight of stairs.

"Come on, then," said Kemp impatiently.

One step at a time, feeling the cold wall with a trembling outstretched hand, I inched my way upwards, glancing behind me, making sure Thomas's outline was still there. My legs were all wobbly and threatening to give way. I bit my lip so hard I tasted blood. I did my best to suppress the panic rising up to drown me, but I'd never been more afraid.

Orford was the first to reach the top. As we followed, a strange crying filled the room. All I wanted to do was to get away from whatever was waiting for us. But what if it was Nyle or Letty? Injured, maybe even dying. Breathless and shaking, I pulled my phone from my pocket, as did my friends from theirs, lighting up the room, which was a small, empty loft. Without warning something charged at us, screeching at such a pitch windows would have shattered if there had been any. All four of us screamed loudly in return, banging into each other to tumble down the stairs and collect in a painful heap at the bottom.

"Letty? Is that you?" asked Kemp, his voice so shaky it sounded like he was singing.

Orford seemed to be the only one that hadn't dropped his phone as he shone it around.

"Evil eyes!" shrieked Thomas.

Orford laughed, then shone his light directly on the creature attached to the *evil eyes*.

"It's a baby goat," said Thomas, with a puff of relief. "I thought it might've been something like that."

"Course you did," said Orford, with a snigger.

"Letty's not here," said Kemp. "I mean, Letty and *Nyle*. You were wrong." His face sagged in disappointment as he rose to his feet to trudge back down the second set of stairs.

I scooped up the frightened little goat, which was actually quite cute, so we could take it back with us. It had obviously found its way in but couldn't find its way out again, poor thing.

"What now?" asked Kemp. His gaze was furious.

"We've got to go back to *The Palace*," I said.

"I'm not going back until I find Letty…and I want *you* to stay away from me," he said, pointing and glaring straight at me. "I'm going on my own."

"Don't blame *me*," I shouted.

"Kemp, it's late, mate. We'll look again tomorrow," said Orford, glancing from Kemp to me with concern.

"Leave me alone!" Kemp screamed back.

The goat jolted in fright, freeing itself from my arms to run off.

"It's your fault," he continued, glaring straight at me again. "If you weren't near us, none of this would have happened. We're all going to be taken and killed because of you."

I stood silent.

"Come on," said Orford. "You're just tired. You can't carry on now. We'll think of something tomorrow. I promise."

Kemp eventually calmed down enough to head back with Orford. I kept my distance, walking behind with Thomas in silence. I hadn't shaken that uneasy feeling that a strange energy lurked on the mountain but I was too tired to mention it, especially with my friends so deflated and irritable. As we approached *The Palace*, Mitchell stood in the courtyard, which was lit up with light sensors.

"Welcome back, kids," he said, crossing his arms across his body. "Nice of you to return."

"I think we might be in trouble," mumbled Thomas.

12

THE CATASTROPHE OF CALLISTUS

"What's going on?" Guru Aabavaana appeared at the door with Mrs Mitchell.

"I'll get Hendrick," Mr Mitchell said, sighing.

"You lot come with me," said his wife, directing us towards the empty dining hall.

"Not her!" yelled Kemp. "I don't want her near me," he continued, advancing towards me, his face red.

Orford stepped in front of me, putting his arms out to shield me. "What's wrong with you, Kemp?"

"Ellery, come with me, please," said Aab.

I followed Aab to the library, which was in total darkness until he turned on a couple of lights by the door. I reckon he brought me here to tell me off the most and the loudest.

"Sit." He smiled.

I sat down waiting for my official rebuke but it never came, not really.

"Your father will be very disappointed with you, Ellery."

"I know, sir. I just wanted to find my friends, sir. They'd do the same for me. Myerscough doesn't understand."

"Why do you call him that? He's your father. He has sacrificed many things for you. I think he deserves more than you are giving him."

I looked down, feeling embarrassed by his truthful words.

"This needs to be left to the adults, not the children, Ellery. We are not dealing with any old person here. Nash will not grant you clemency because you are only a teenager. He has no morals, no principals. He will do whatever it takes to get what he wants. Do you understand this?"

"Yes, sir…but it's not fair," I began, placing my hands together in namaste, as I felt the anger rising within me. "Why should Nash be able to take all my friends, to make me angry, to connect to my energy and kill me and yet I can't do the same to him? It's just not fair." I wiped away the tears from my face with the back of my hand.

"Why can't you do the same?" asked Aab.

"Pardon?"

"Why can you not do the same to Nash?" he repeated, his caterpillar eyebrows meeting in the middle.

"Because if I try to connect to his negative energy it would be so much greater than mine, and I wouldn't stand a chance."

"I see," said Aab, stroking his beard. "I think perhaps you have misinterpreted how this works."

"I don't understand, sir."

"Clearly. When an ebonoid tries to take the power of another, he or she is not taking negative energy, only spirit energy. Whatever he or she decides to do with it, be it positive or negative, is up to him or her."

"I'm not sure what you mean, sir. Myerscough – I mean, my father – told me that if Nash could latch onto the negative part of my life force, then that would finish me off."

"Hmmm. I think latching onto *any* part of your life force would finish you off. I suspect his over-simplified explanation was to keep you safe from Nash. Your father loves you very much, Ellery."

"You mean he lied to me?"

"No, it's more of a sugar-coated explanation and perhaps the only way he thought he could protect not only you, but all of us. If Nash acquires the spirit of yet another ebonoid, his power would be insurmountable with cataclysmic consequences."

I clenched my jaws tightly together.

"I need the truth, sir. The truth without the sugar-coating, please."

"Yes, Ellery, you do. Nash wants to make you as angry as he possibly can so that all the anger you produce will turn into physical negative energy, leaving very little energy within you. This makes it easy for him to then attach to the small amount of energy left within your spirit, and remove it. That is why he had difficulty last year at Quinton House. You didn't produce enough negative energy, so you had lots of power still within your spirit that he couldn't latch on to. He was used to fighting rage with more rage, which is not what you gave him, it seems."

"So he's not attaching to my negative energy?"

"No, that's all produced physically, outside of you. He can't attach to that. I think you are confusing life force with energy. Your life force is like a ball. You've been taught to turn it around from negative to positive to redirect your temper. Am I correct?"

"Yes, sir. Dave taught me last year."

"This gives you focus and it also gives you time to refrain from losing your temper. It is an excellent exercise. However, this 'ball' – your life force – is your spirit, made up of both positive and negative energy. It is not separated but combined. If you release negative energy out into the physical world, it weakens your life force."

"So why isn't Nash weak, then? He's producing tonnes of negativity all the time."

"Yes, he is, but he has two life forces. He acquired the ebonoid spirit of another some years ago. This means that although he weakens each time he is negative, he has so much in reserve that the effect is negligible. This is why you must not try to use your energy in the same way that he does. You cannot win this way."

I had too many thoughts bouncing around my head. If only I could have told Nyle and Letty about them.

"Have you ever heard the story of the gifted twins, Benvolio and Blaze, sons of King Callistus?"

"No, sir."

"It's an old Magaecian legend – probably in this library here somewhere. Benvolio and Blaze were *gifted*. It does not say exactly how, but I think you might be able to work that out as their skills were not dissimilar to your own."

"There you are," growled Myerscough, stomping through the door before Aab could tell me the rest of the story.

"I thought you left the island," I said curtly.

"You wish," he snapped. "We missed the last ferry."

"I'll leave you to it," said Aab, getting up from his chair.

My heart sped up, not at the thought of the rollicking I was about to get from Myerscough, but at the contempt I harboured inside, now that I was aware he'd treated me like a baby, keeping the truth from me.

"It's been a tough night, Hendrick," said Aab softly. "We've had a long chat and Ellery's promised me she will get a good story from the library here tomorrow to keep her out of mischief. Perhaps her friends should do the same." He winked at me, then left.

Myerscough nodded, accompanied with a grunt. "I'm too tired to argue with you now," he said. "We'll talk about this tomorrow."

***

Straight after breakfast, Orford, Thomas and I sprinted to the library. We were meant to have a double period of totems with Mitchell, but he'd gone off with Myerscough to the mainland so we were allowed a couple of frees. I wasn't surprised that Kemp hadn't come with us.

"What did Mrs Mitchell say to you last night?" I asked.

"After the shouting?" said Thomas.

"Actually, she gave us a detention. She said we'd have to look up the relevance of the goat totem. The kid must've come to us for a reason," said Orford.

"What kid?" asked Thomas. "We were the only kids there last night."

"A baby goat's called a kid, Thomas," said Orford, rolling his eyes.

"Oh, yeah. I forgot."

"I hadn't thought about the goat," I said. "Why don't you look for books on goat totems, while Thomas and I look for Magaecian myths and legends," I suggested.

We spent ages finding the right books. The librarian seemed to have a weird filing system which none of us could understand. Orford had a totem book to look at, *Why That Totem?* by Annie Malshifter. I had Kaminsky and Bing's *Magaecian Fables, Myths and Legends*, the abridged version, which was still enormous. I'm not sure what Thomas found – he'd already sat down and started to read.

"Goats mean it's time to stretch yourself," said Orford, who was the first to break the silence as he flicked through the pages of his library book. "It says to allow yourself to reach your goals. Believe in your power – the only one who can stop you is yourself."

"This one's good," interrupted Thomas, pointing out the title of his book: *Mysteries at Manburgh Castle* by Terry Fiyed.

"What's that got to do with Magaecian legends?" puffed Orford, obviously losing patience.

Thomas let out a blast of giggles.

"What's so funny?" snapped Orford.

"It says here that Lord Caldwell Nutter gifted Manburgh Castle to Sir Farley Fernsby of Prickly Bottom near Dorset."

"Lord Nutter? Prickly Bottom?" said Orford. "Stop messing about. We need to concentrate."

"But it says here…"

"Shhhhh."

I couldn't find any stories called "Benvolio and Blaze" but there was one called *The Catastrophe of Callistus*. Aab had mentioned the name Callistus so maybe this was the one. I took the book and sat down to read.

When King Callistus's wife, Adrianna, died in childbirth, she left her husband to care for their twin boys, Benvolio and Blaze. The boys were identical in appearance but their temperaments could not be more opposed. Blaze, like his name, was likened to pure sunshine – a blazing brightness, kind and caring, while Benvolio was sullen, sombre and wrathful.

On reaching a decade and three, it became apparent that the boys had been blessed with the powers of Magae. Callistus went to great pains to stress the responsibilities that came with Magae's gifts. Used wisely, the future would be bright and the kingdom would flourish; used without discretion, it would all but wither and die. Callistus educated the younglings as best he could, seeking advice from Magaecian gurus from far and wide on how best to instruct his sons. Although he knew the boys were total opposites, he thought this made them all the more suitable to create a successful kingdom, uniting both positive and negative points of view.

Whilst Blaze had a talent for resolving disagreements and uniting his friends, Benvolio was void of empathy and unable to see any way but his own way. Always on the side of pessimism, never on the side of optimism, Benvolio's mood grew darker and a dubious energy grew along with it. When Callistus was killed in combat, the throne was passed down to the twins. Still under advisement from Magaecian gurus, Blaze studied hard but Benvolio refused to do the same. Blaze respected his enemies as well as his friends; his elders and his subjects, but Benvolio showed only disregard for everyone, scorning anyone that crossed his path in a hurricane of prevailing fear. He threw tantrums on a regular basis, receiving only the answers he wished to hear from his frightened advisers who knew they'd have to suffer the pain of his power should they disagree.

Blaze's popularity provoked his brother, prompting Benvolio to hatch a sinister plan. He sought counsel with an evil hag who taught him the art of shapeshifting. Mastering a shift into a terrible lizard-like creature with venomous drool from emerald sacs behind his sword-like teeth, the hag collected the poisonous slime that would slowly sap the life from Benvolio's unwanted brother. Only then, when he was at his weakest, could Benvolio absorb the spirit of his twin containing Magae's power, so that he had twice the energy to rule not just his own kingdom but many.

After several moons, and sacs of poison, Benvolio approached his ailing twin, too weak to stand without aide. Poor Blaze knew he had little time remaining on Magae and felt sorry his brother saw only the bad in everything, never acting on what was good with the world but instead with what was not.

"Why do you try to connect to me, brother?" asked Blaze. "You will die."

"Not I, dear brother, but you," replied Benvolio.

"If you had studied as I have done, you would know that connecting to a spirit that lies near to its death means that in union you will die too."

"No!" cried out Benvolio, with such rage at his oversight it brought about a frenzied energy that was so powerful it stopped the birds from chirping and blotted out the sun. His anger could not be contained, growing ever more with each breath until he shapeshifted into a hideous creature.

Subjects sought safety with haste from such a monstrous sight, but Blaze saw only his brother, not the beast he'd become. He saw the boy with whom he'd shared his life. He knew in his good heart that they *must both return their gifts to Magae if they were to save and restore and protect their kingdom. This, perchance, was his only possibility to attach and remove Benvolio's spirit whilst at its weakest, depleted of the negative power he'd subconsciously released in his rage. So, taking his last breath, Blaze found his brother's spirit to conjoin, removing them both from the world to become one with Magae. Thunder struck and an icy wind grew stronger, lashing at the palace gardens, bubbling up the seas of yonder. Hailstones battered the lifeless bodies of the twins as if to pound away all energies of darkness.*

A sudden silence filled the kingdom and with the power of magaec the blackness lifted. The sun shone more brightly than ever it had before and the birds returned to chirp new songs of freedom. The kingdom rejoiced, and peace and democracy reigned once more therein. Magae had gained twin spirits within her soul. Benvolio became one with the soil, condemned to the dark but offered a chance to see the light in the form of a tree. Blaze could be seen every day high up in the heavens as part of the sun's rays, so necessary for existence of any life on Magae.

It was said that even Magae herself learned a lesson from this tale – she ne'er bestowed her gifts twice at once thereafter.

I looked over the book to see Orford and Thomas still flicking through the pages of their books.

"According to this, I've got to make Nash angrier than he's ever been before," I said.

"Why?" asked Thomas.

"To make him weak. When he's weak, I've got a chance to take his spirit energy. If Nash releases all of his negativity in one go, that should leave very little energy within him. It's the only time I'd be able to attach and remove his life force."

"But how can you make him that angry?" said Orford.

"That's the problem," I answered with a huge sigh. "I can't. Aab told me not to take that path because I'd never be able to defeat him that way."

"What if you tell Nash he smells?" suggested Thomas. "Or that his totem smells – that should do it."

"I seriously doubt it." Orford laughed.

"Kick him in the goolies, then," said Thomas, jumping to his feet to demonstrate a kick in mid-air.

"Goolies?" repeated Orford, letting out a hysterical laugh that echoed through the library. "Who are you, best mates with Charles Dickens?"

I let out a splutter. A wide smile spread across Thomas's face, turning into an infectious belly laugh. It felt so good.

As we got up to leave for our next lesson, I offered to put all three library books back. Thomas's book lay open at Chapter Four – "The Hidden Sepulchre of Manburgh".

"Where is this place, Thomas?" I asked.

"Its whereabouts are a mystery." He giggled. "That's why it's in the book – *Mysteries of Manburgh Castle*."

"Why didn't you show us this before, you dufus," shouted Orford, observing the page.

"You said you wanted to concentrate."

"I meant—"

"Okay, okay. Nash could have Nyle in there, Thomas," I said.

"And Letty," said Orford, shooting me a furious glance.

"Of course." I nodded. "How are we going to find this hidden sepulchre?"

"I keep telling you," said Thomas. "Its whereabouts are a mystery."

"It could be anywhere," added Orford.

"And there *is* a place called Prickly Bottom, by the way. I've just looked it up on my phone," muttered Thomas under his breath.

Our thoughts were interrupted by Delia who ran into the library. She was hysterical, flailing her arms about.

"Kemp's missing!" she said, trying to catch her breath. "He went looking for Letty and didn't come back. Myerscough and Mitchell have arranged another search party."

Delia's words filled the air like a cymbal crash.

"We've got to find that sepulchre," said Orford.

13

THE SPELL

We waited until the weekend before making our way to the old church and abbey ruins by the cemetery. This was not out of bounds so we decided a visit during daylight hours would be far less creepy than a night jaunt, plus there was the added advantage that we couldn't get expelled for being there.

The ruined walls of the abbey were like a pile of masonry after my dragon debut last term. Collapsed walls, columns broken and toppled, and the cemetery's iron gates had been left to balance against the only solid-looking wall. Weeds spread like disease through the cracked stone, threatening to topple more of the old foundations as we clambered over loose debris.

Standing still in the ancient grounds, I sensed an underlying angst that there was an energy, a force beneath, that I could not explain. No matter how hard we looked, no matter how many stones we turned, we came up with a big, fat nothing.

"Maybe there's a secret opening, a hidden gateway or door or something," suggested Orford.

"If that were true," I said, "we'd have found it. We've searched literally everywhere."

We'd searched all day, behind the church ruins, pushing cemetery headstones, hoping to reveal a secret path or hidden tunnel.

"What exactly is a sepulchre?" asked Thomas.

"It's an underground tomb, kind of thing," said Orford, hardly looking at Thomas, too busy digging up areas he thought would magic up a doorway.

"Does it have to be under the old, ruined church?" asked Thomas, holding his chin in his hands. "Perhaps it's just near it."

"I don't know," I said, sounding quite snappy. The frustration was getting to me. "Sepulchres are usually attached to a church, aren't they?"

Thomas shrugged.

"This is hopeless," I said. "We should go back."

"Are we just going to let him kidnap us all?" asked Thomas.

"No!" I yelled, causing both boys to grab their chests. "I'm sorry. It's just…I feel like we're getting nowhere."

"All right, Ellery. Keep your hair on," replied Orford. "You've got to stop getting so uptight."

"That's easy for you to say."

"Yes, it is. Nash is going to find it far too easy to get you annoyed if you're already angry about something like this."

"Shut up!" I retorted, turning on my heels in the direction of the main building. It was useless and on top of that, Orford was right. I didn't want to tell him that, of course, but I was beginning to panic at the prospect that Nash would get my energy far too easily.

We got back in time for dinner, barely talking to each other throughout the meal.

"We'll work it out," said Orford.

"No," I said, shoving back my chair as I got up from the table. "You need to keep away from me...both of you."

"No, Ellery," said Orford, grabbing my wrist, gazing up at me with his grey-blue eyes. "That's what he wants. Don't give him what he wants. United we stand, divided we fall."

"The Three Musketeers?" said Thomas. "Dad and I saw it at the cinema once."

Orford nodded.

"Hey! That's us," said Thomas. "The Three Musketeers. All for one and one for all!"

I smiled.

Orford rose up beside me, slipping his hand into mine. An awkward silence prevailed as his gaze lingered. I felt the heat rush to my cheeks and resorted to staring at the floor until Thomas placed his hand on top of ours like he was about to give a team talk.

"See you in the morning for Forest Protection with Lameko," said Thomas, removing his hand to take his plate up.

Orford and I broke apart, producing forced smiles of embarrassment before leaving too.

***

As I slouched over my books in Lameko's class, a scrappy piece of paper landed by my book. *Have you come up with any ideas to send Nash into a crazy frenzy yet or will we have to resort to Master Dickens's "goolies" plan?* I chuckled to myself at Orford's note.

"Ellery? Any thoughts?" asked Mr Lameko, obviously observing the glazed look I must have acquired, switching off from his lesson ages ago.

I hadn't a clue what he'd asked me, so I just shook my head in a hope he'd move on to someone else who was actually listening. He did.

A bell rang to signal break time, creating a cacophony of scraping chairs and noisy chatter. I was the last apart from Orford to get up off my chair. Orford stood in front of a poster Lameko had hung up in class about the Queen's Commonwealth Canopy, a project launched some years ago. It was an appeal to all fifty-three Commonwealth nations to contribute areas of indigenous forest to be permanently preserved. It was set up to bring about real change for generations to come. At least something good was happening in the world, I suppose.

"You've got to think of something, Ellery. It's no good hiding behind your temper," said Orford.

"What temper?" I shot back.

Orford didn't answer, merely raising his eyebrows sarcastically.

"It's a puberty thing," I said, instantly wishing I hadn't let those words free.

163

Orford's face flushed.

"All teenagers go through it. It's part of growing up," I said, making it worse.

"For normal teenagers maybe, but not ebonoid ones," replied Orford, with a smile. "You can't let rip like the rest of us."

"I know. I'm finding it really hard to be positive all the time. I want to be in a bad mood sometimes."

Orford gazed at me, caressing me with his eyes. I reached for my hair and started playing with the loose tendrils that had escaped from my ponytail. My brain turned all foggy and I didn't know what to say. I focused on an ink stain on the floor, staring so hard it changed shape.

"What are you doing in here?" asked Ashkii Mitchell, who was at the door, his hand firmly entwined in Radella Tewksbury's. I reckon he was going to snog her.

"We were just leaving," said Orford, wrenching his eyes away from Radella's bust which he was unsubtly ogling.

"Ash?" I asked. "Do you know anything about the hidden sepulchre here?"

"There's no hidden sepulchre but there are prisoners' tombs," said Radella. "They're under the cells. We tried to go for a smoke in there the first week of school but Chef MacBrennan caught us before we'd even got to the cemetery. She was so mad. We weren't allowed donk for a week."

"You smoke?" said Orford.

"How do you get into the tombs?" I butted in.

"You'll get into trouble. I wouldn't advise it," she continued.

"I just want to see it. That's all," I added as light-heartedly as I could. "I'm doing a project on ancient burial grounds and stuff."

Orford raised his eyebrows at my lie which seemed to slip out far too easily. Radella narrowed her eyes at both of us with a shrug.

"I can take you, if you like. It would have to be at night though, otherwise we'll get caught for sure. You'll be disappointed. It's not meant to be all that interesting. Last year's lot said it smelled of mildew and rotting flesh. It might be too scary for you two."

"I'll come too," suggested Ash, trying his utmost to appear chivalrous but pulling a face suggesting otherwise.

Orford raised his eyebrows at me and smiled.

"We'll have to tell Thomas," I said.

"I'm not some sort of babysitter," said Radella. "You can't invite your whole class."

"It's just one more person. He's fine. Very brave," I said.

Ash and Radella started French kissing, prompting us to leave the classroom ASAP and head for our common room. On the way there, I had a sudden loss of confidence, so many *what ifs* going through my mind.

"Orford," I began.

"What?"

"If Nash really is in the tombs under the cells...if he's there tonight..." I said, summoning a deep breath before continuing. "I think we—"

"Should tell Radella and Ash," he interrupted. "I was thinking that too."

"No...I mean, yes, but I wasn't actually thinking that."

"What then?"

"I was thinking…we should have a plan B."

"Plan B? What's plan B? Let me guess. You're going to tell me not to come tonight so that I don't get killed and then, when you find our friends, you can take all the glory."

"What do you mean? No – it's not that, you idiot. Why would you say that? It's always about ego with you."

"What's plan B, then?" asked Orford, loosening his collar.

"It's sort of a backup plan – if it all goes wrong."

"Great. Now I'm filled with confidence."

"If Nash forces me to lose my temper…"

"You mustn't let him, Ellery."

"Orford, let's face it – I can't help it. It's going to be too easy for him to get the better of me. I'll try my best – you know I will, but I'm just being realistic here."

Orford didn't answer, which kind of said it all. He must've been thinking the same even if he hadn't said it aloud. My insides filled with uncertainty mixed in with a mild panic at what probable end awaited once Nash had overpowered me.

"If I can't help it, then he'll take my spirit energy, my life force, and that will kill me…"

"Ellery!"

"Hear me out, Orford. It will kill me, so I reckon he'll take my dragon first. We have to stop him."

"What are you saying? You can't murder him – that would make you as bad as he is. You'll become Nash. You'll never be able to control the negativity it will bring you."

"I know that. I'm not suggesting I murder *him*, I'm just saying that if he takes my dragon, then it's going to be up to *you* to kill it."

"*Me*? I'm not killing your totem."

"It won't be my totem, it will be Nash's."

"No!"

"The only way to kill a dragon is to cut off its head or to stab it in the heart. That's what Myerscough said. You have to do this, Orford. If Nash gets the dragon, we're all doomed. You know that. That's why you've got to be armed and ready to attack should you need to."

"With what, exactly? My pencil? Or maybe I can use my new compass!"

"I've got an idea for that. Lameko leaves a pair of garden shears by the cemetery. They're quite big and extremely sharp. You can pick them up on the way tonight."

"Thanks, can't wait. Sounds like I'm in for a spectacular evening," spat Orford, his jaw tightly clenched.

"Have you got a better idea, then?"

"Actually," replied Orford with a smirk. "I might have."

"Go on, then. I'm all ears."

"Maybe we've been looking at this from the wrong angle."

"What angle?"

"We're looking at this from Nash's point of view instead of from ours."

"You've lost me. You said we needed to think more like Nash."

"We do to find our friends, but acting like Nash would mean making him the angriest he's ever been. It's not possible. Like Aab said, we won't be able to make him angry enough."

"I know what makes him angry," I said. "Dwellers. The way they've treated and wrecked the planet, draining Magae of all reserves. All the dreadful things that come with climate change like pollution, higher temperatures, melted polar ice caps, deforestation, loss of animal and plant diversity…"

"Okay, okay. I get it. No need for the lecture," said Orford, gripping his throat. "The point is, you're angry about this too, so that's not going to work."

"And?"

"And…maybe you've got to get him to see it from another perspective. There's still hope. The Queen's Commonwealth Canopy is a brilliant project for one. We're trying to put things right as humans, not as Dwellers or Magaecians. Mankind is trying to create a lower carbon footprint; we're trying to clean up our plastic and use less of it. We're awesome humans, like Aab said, with incredible brains, which is why we're striving to create answers so that we won't ruin the planet. Electric cars and someday electric planes, or maybe someone will invent a truck that runs on orange juice! And then we've got lots more Dwellers eating a lot less meat and more plant-based food. The point is, there's hope, Ellery, so long as we focus on the good stuff – and not on the bad. You've got to be positive because that's what gives you power over Nash. A sort of *own the positive and lose the negative*, kind of spell."

"That's a good spell," I said. "I'm not sure Nash will see it that way, though."

"You've got to change his point of view, like Darwin Burgess tried to do. Just remember, a totem chooses you for a reason. The dragon hasn't come to you so that you can get your own way all the time, and lash out like a two-year-old. It's to give you—"

"I know – courage, strength and fortitude – whatever that means," I said, gesturing like a Shakespearean actor.

"Exactly. Dragons are messengers of balance, masters of the elements and providers of protection. It's with you to guide you. Nash wants to use it like a weapon. You can't do the same. You won't. All those books you've got on totems and dragons – it's all in there. We've all read them with you. It's going to be fine."

"Okay…" I nodded, although my stomach said otherwise, churning uncomfortably. "We still need to find that underground tomb, though, if we want to get our friends back."

"I know, but if our friends aren't there with Nash, then I don't know where they can be. There's nowhere left. Perhaps he *has* left the island after all."

"No," I replied. "He's definitely here. I can feel him."

Delia suddenly barged past me to catch up with Angela Yin who was outside waving. She accidentally nudged me straight into Orford, causing me to inadvertently fall into his arms. He turned abruptly and stared straight into my eyes, holding them hostage. My skin was invaded by goosebumps as I felt his heart thumping beneath his jumper.

"Right, then," he said, with an expression marring his face as if he'd been told he'd been removed from the school Magupe team. "I…I…erm…see you later," he slurred before sprinting away.

I continued to the common room in search of Thomas to discuss our new plan. I knew he'd love the spell – *own the positive and lose the negative*.

14

WALKING THE PLANK

Before I got changed to meet the others, I checked myself out in the mirror in my bra and pants. All my friends had bigger boobs than me. It wasn't fair. I still looked like a little girl. Letty always received admiring looks from boys. I paused. I really missed my friend. We shared a bedroom here at *The Palace*. Most of the rooms had two beds in them, but some had three and I think one had four beds. All the Year 12s had their own private bedrooms – something I'd involuntarily acquired now that Letty was gone. I paused again. I'd have given anything to have her back. I examined myself in the mirror again as if my boobs might've grown in the few minutes I'd been standing there. Nope. Still peanuts. I took a pair of socks from my drawer and folded each one before stuffing them into each bra cup. I tried a T-shirt on top and smiled at my new, quite sexy form. I took one more pair of socks to add to the padding. This was definitely overkill. Before I had a chance to remove them, there was a soft knock on the door.

"Ready?" whispered Orford, creaking open the door to peep his head round.

"Of course," I said, thrusting down my T-shirt over my new massive boobs, before shoving a sweatshirt over the top as quickly as I possibly could. I threw on a fleece and then my anorak on top of that to make doubly sure I'd covered them up. He smiled at me. I'm not sure if it was a flirtatious smile or a *what the hell?* kind of smile.

We met Ash and Radella by the cemetery. The cold wind stung my face, howling like a wolf as it tore through the old ruin walls. Radella, Ash, Orford and I were dressed in black and grey but Thomas turned up in a bright yellow anorak. It was too late to send him back so I didn't comment and neither did the others, although Radella rolled her eyes a bit too obviously. Orford opened his rucksack in front of me to reveal the pair of gardening shears which now didn't look as large as I'd remembered.

"Come on. Are we going or not?" said Radella, jerking her head in the direction she wanted us to go.

"Radella," I began. "I think you ought to know that Nash might be in these tombs. If you'd rather not come, just give us the directions instead. Perhaps you should head back anyway to let the teachers know where we are in case something happens."

"I'm not scared," replied Radella, looking slightly excited. "Besides, if Nash isn't there, we'll get into real trouble telling the teachers. Let's just get on with it and make a run for it if things get out of hand."

Ash looked particularly anxious and was noticeably quiet before mumbling something under his breath. I guessed, probably something like, *my dad will kill me.*

"Lead the way," I said. I looked briefly over at Orford, who was chewing the side of his mouth. His face was so pale all the blood must have left it to sink down to his ankles, making him very fidgety.

We followed Radella and Ash to the eerie prison cell block. Radella walked confidently on, passing the woods and then zigzagging down the mountain along a path which gradually disappeared. About halfway down, Radella pushed aside some thorns and creepers revealing an icy track, glinting in the frost. It looked like a route time had forgotten, behind thick and tangled bushes.

"Be careful here," she said. "It's slippery."

We followed Radella, scrambling over wobbly, uneven rocks, clambering on top of enormous ankle-twisting boulders. It was so cold my teeth began to chatter. I lost concentration and misplaced my foot, sending a mass of loose stones tumbling over the rock face. Orford grabbed my scarf to steady me, almost throttling me in the process.

"Sorry," he said, loosening his grip, then tucking my scarf back into my anorak. He touched my neck. A warm feeling passed through me and I felt myself blushing. Luckily it was too dark for him to see.

"It's through this gap," puffed Radella.

We edged our way through to find ourselves facing an unexpected opening to a cave. This seemed like a long way from the prison cells. Maybe the entrance was purposely far away for safety and secrecy during wartime and we'd have to follow it a long way round before it would bring us back to underneath the cells; or maybe Radella didn't have a clue where she was going and was just showing off to impress Ash. No one else appeared to doubt her route so I kept quiet.

"We're not going in there, are we?" said Thomas. "It looks like a black hole."

Radella didn't answer but continued through the opening. It was impenetrably dark and cold inside. The wind moaned against the cave entrance, sending in creepy coils of mist to welcome us. My eyes took ages to adjust to the dark before I could make out shapes. Giant stalactites of ice hung from above like a crystal chandelier. Thomas was right, it was like being sucked into a black hole as we edged our way further into the cave.

We used our phone torches to give us some light, but it didn't make me feel any less scared. Every step seemed to echo in the freezing air which smelled of decay and gone-off water. I swallowed a couple of deep breaths as every muscle in my body tensed involuntarily. As we continued warily, it narrowed into a chamber, lower and lower, less and less space until we had to crawl on our hands and knees.

"Are you sure this is right?" asked Thomas.

Orford struggled with his backpack. He had to remove it and stuff the shears down the back of his trousers.

"I hope I don't cut off something important," he whispered.

I felt breathless. Perhaps I was claustrophobic. Perhaps we were running out of air. It felt all wrong. Maybe this was a trap and we should have turned back.

"I've got pins and needles," said Thomas.

We carried on for ages, mostly in silence before Radella made an announcement.

"Uh-oh! There's a slight problem."

"No way!" shrieked Ash, looking past her at the sudden drop into unknown blackness.

A thick, unstable-looking wooden plank stretched over the deep chasm, so cavernous you couldn't see to the bottom of it. Unless we turned back, there was nowhere else we could go but forward, which meant we'd have to walk the plank.

My suspicions about Radella's route were disturbingly correct. I doubt she'd been here before, or indeed anywhere near the old prisoners' tombs – *ever*. As we contemplated giving up, a sudden blood-curdling scream rang out from the other side of the crater.

"That's Letty," I said. "Surely there must be another way of getting across." I searched Radella's face for answers but she had none; instead she simply shrugged. Why had I even asked her? She clearly knew no more than I did.

"We've got to go across," said Thomas. "We've got to save our friends, Ellery."

He was right, but why did it have to be such a drop? Why couldn't Nash have taken and hidden our friends in a house or a bungalow?

"I'm going, no matter what. Anyone else coming?" said Thomas, squaring his shoulders like a mighty warrior.

"We're all coming," said Orford, looking at Ash and Radella, whose faces said otherwise. "I'll go first. You come behind me, Ellery, then Thomas behind you."

Orford squeezed past Radella to crawl over and onto the plank. I followed, then Thomas. Ash and Radella were pretty much frozen to the spot, and who could blame them?

"You two stay," I said. "It might be too much weight with all of us on the plank in one go."

Ash nodded frantically, obviously relieved at my suggestion.

As Orford crawled agonisingly slowly in front of me, desperately trying to keep his balance, I held my breath. With the heavy shears still in his trousers, he began to struggle, his hips bouncing from side to side as the shears shifted weight with each movement, slowly edging their way further up his back to release themselves from his trousers, straight out and down into the abyss. He lost his balance and slipped, hanging there by his fingertips, legs flailing as he struggled not to let go. It was like the Quinton House tunnel all over again, only worse. I tried to inch my way closer towards him but the plank reverberated with every tremble, creaking unnervingly to send a personal shot of adrenaline to urge me to respond with the flight instinct. I shook my head to remove negative thoughts and forced myself to look only at Orford and not at the dark vision below me, threatening to reach out and grab me before pulling me down to my end.

Don't look down. Don't look down, I kept telling myself over and over. Gingerly, I attempted to sit astride the plank on my bottom, my legs hanging over either side like riding a broad shire horse, but it was far more difficult than I thought. My weight kept shifting too much to one side and I went veering over to the left, heading off the plank terrifyingly fast – stopped in the nick of time by Thomas behind me, who heroically grabbed my trousers by the waist as well as some of my skin, I might add, to yank me back upright.

"Thank you," I spluttered, practically swallowing my words. I knew he'd risked falling too by doing that and I was more grateful than he'd ever know. I took a deep breath. It was intensely uncomfortable sitting this way, particularly as I was not at all a bendy or flexible person. Gymnastics was not my forte and never would be. The circulation was fast cutting off around my legs and feet.

"It's okay, Orford," I said, my voice far higher than usual. "We've got this."

As the words left my mouth, one of his hands slipped off the plank. We didn't have this, not in the slightest. I breathed deeply to stop the panic rising up to strangle me. I'd saved him once before, on the beach. I could do it again, I knew I could. As I struggled, failing to keep the panic at bay, my tongue tingled. It was then that I knew I had my elemental energy. It was a sign. It always tingled just before I had a surge of elemental force. As Orford could do nothing but let go, I used the elements within him, the minerals, the water, the air in his lungs to somehow latch onto an energy flowing through me. I brought my hands together with a clap, producing a whirl around us both, like a captured storm. I then pushed at the air in front of me, focusing as best I could on the other side of the plank to safety. We shot like two stones from a catapult, smashing into the wall with a painful crash. Several boulders loosened up, showering down to crack the plank crisply into two separate pieces, straight down into the blackness beneath…taking Thomas with it!

"Thomas!" I howled. "Thomas!" I fell to my knees, my insides emptier than the void that had just devoured my friend. I felt my spirit shrink as I cried out his name again. I crawled to the edge, looking over, screaming Thomas's name like a wild animal.

"Maybe he's fallen onto a shelf."

"He's gone, Ellery," said Orford, softly.

"But he could be clinging on somewhere."

"He's gone."

I closed my eyes, only to see Thomas falling again in my mind. My stomach twisted and tightened as I collapsed in a sobbing heap onto the ice-cold floor.

"Go for help!" yelled Orford across to Ash and Radella.

Ash's arms flew up in distress before coming down to grip his head like a maniac. Radella didn't answer but raised her hand up to us calmly, comforting Ash before retreating back with him the way they'd come.

"Are you okay?" asked Orford, stumbling to his feet, obviously winded and bruised with numerous cuts bleeding from his head and hands. He tried to walk but he'd hurt his knee. He winced as he lifted his joggers to see the damage. It was bloody and swollen.

"I should have saved him," I whimpered. "I could have..."

"No. You couldn't," said Orford, slipping to the floor, sliding over to hold me tightly as I sobbed.

"Kemp was right. You should have kept away from me – all of you. I can't do this, Orford."

"Yes, you can. The dragon totem will give you strength and courage..."

"*When?*" I screamed at Orford, causing him to grasp his throat.

"I'm not going to lie to you, Ellery. It's going to get far worse than this. Nash will most likely torture us all in a cruel and gruesome way, so comfort yourself in the knowledge that Thomas has got off lightly. We've got to carry on and find our friends, our fat friends, and you've got to try to reason with Nash otherwise it will never end. It's all or nothing. It's the only chance we'll have. We've got to at least try – it's what Thomas would have wanted. Together we're strong, alone you're weak. United we stand, divided we fall."

"All for one and one for all." I sniffed in between hyperventilated breaths.

Orford cried too. He leaned into my face, gazing so intensely into my eyes as if looking straight through to my injured soul. He pressed his lips against my own to ignite a hint of hope within my spirit, stirring a new desire to survive.

As he moved, he squealed.

"You're injured," I said, removing my scarf to wrap it round his wounded knee.

"Gross," he said. "Your taste in scarves is horrible."

"Shut up." I sniffed.

"I'm sorry about the shears, Ellery. If I hadn't brought them, Thomas…"

"If I hadn't told you to bring them, Thomas…"

"It's okay…*super-swirl mega-girl!*"

The last thing I felt was *super*. I helped Orford up to limp through an opening which was much bigger than the way we'd come. It was more like a cavern with room to stand. The smell was unpleasant, mildewy and rotten. I could imagine dead bodies in here. I only hoped mine wouldn't become one of them. As Orford got some momentum, able to manage more weight on his knee, we were surrounded by a dreadful stench of rotting plants and an unidentifiable foul odour. In fact, it was beginning to resemble the obnoxious smell I'd encountered that night at Quinton House when the wyrm came to visit me. I began to wretch.

"It's mind over matter," said Orford. "Think of a smell you like and imagine it flowing through your nostrils."

I immediately thought of mint. It wasn't an instant remedy but it was helpful in stopping me from gagging.

There seemed to be a lighter area through the rocks ahead of us. As we headed towards it, a weird sensation told me we were in real danger. Something moved within the shadows. I grabbed Orford, pulling him back to move into a darker space to hide. My phone torch picked an inopportune moment to give up on me, and Orford's had gone overboard with the garden shears. We were now plunged into darkness save for the shafts of light coming through the rocks. Every instinct told me not to move. I signalled to Orford not to make a sound but I'm not sure if he saw me. Desperately trying to see through the gloom, my eyes flickered from side to side. A sudden shift in the shadows prompted me to jump up from the spot but before I could move, a large hand grabbed me from behind and somebody else grabbed Orford too. Whoever was behind me wrenched my arms viciously in some kind of lock. Orford caught a hard jab in his ribs as he tried to resist.

Rage rose up from the pit of my stomach to form a hard lump in my throat as I lashed out with my feet. Orford tried to signal a *no* with his head but it was too late. The man dropped me to hold his throat which I'd probably closed up with ebonoid energy.

"You're releasing all your negativity," spat Orford. "It makes you weak. Don't make it so easy for him."

Orford received another severe rebuke, this time in the form of a spiteful, full-thrusted smack in the face, sending him unsteadily backwards and down onto the ground as his knees buckled beneath him. The man hoisted him up roughly. The other man just stood there in front of me not knowing what to do next.

"We'll come with you," I said firmly. Just put him down or I'll hurt you – both of you – like Nash hurts you. You know that I can. One of you can walk ahead and the other behind. We won't run off. You have our word." I'm not sure what I expected these men to do but they agreed. I knew I wouldn't use my negative energy but I suppose they didn't know that. The man holding Orford put him down to let us walk between the two of them.

"Regain your composure and don't think like Nash," Orford whispered in my ear.

I nodded. At least I think I nodded, my whole body was trembling.

Both men were large and muscular and didn't utter a word. The man in front led us to a clearing, while the other stayed close behind us. We reached a fire-lit entrance to a large underground vault, the Manburgh Prison coat of arms emblazoned in the stone walls. It was a familiar place. I knew I'd never been here before and yet I'd seen it. I'd seen it in my dreams. It must have meant something but I had no time to analyse it, confronted abruptly by a devastating sight ahead of me. A row of six tombs. On top of the three central tombs, three tortured bodies, spasmodically flinching, bound and gagged. Nyle, Letty and Kemp.

I failed to fight back the tears as I covered my mouth with my hands and sobbed. I felt my spirit shrivel some more.

"Own the positive, lose the negative." Orford sent a silent spell to me. *"They're alive,"* he continued. *"This is the positive. Don't give up yet."*

I swallowed my salty tears dropping over my lips and gave a subtle nod once again, followed by a sharp intake of breath.

A man strode in from an opening behind the tombs. An unpleasant, intimidating energy emanated from him. I could feel it straight through to my bones. It was cruel and foreboding. It was Saxon Nash. Orford's hand suddenly grasped mine.

"Here," he whispered, placing something in my shaky hand. It was my dragon totem stone. We clutched it together, hand in hand.

"Hello, kids," said Nash, with a sarcastic smile. "Welcome to the party."

I could hear Orford's heavy breathing as he tightened his grip round my hand.

"You took your time, young Orford. I thought you'd bring her to me ages ago."

I pulled my hand away from Orford's, dropping the stone to the ground.

"Didn't he tell you, Ellery? He's not on your side, he's on *mine*."

15

THE WYRM THAT TURNED

I felt my jaw physically drop at his conceited statement.

"I'm not on your side!" yelled Orford at Nash, before turning to me. "He's taunting you. Whatever he says, don't react. He wants you to lose your temper. Please don't do it. Own it."

Orford was right. Nash knew how to push all the right buttons. I was angry and also disappointed for allowing myself, for just a split second, to think Orford had double-crossed me. I didn't want to panic but I was afraid. So afraid. I was way out of my depth here.

Nash sent out a huge bolt of ebonoid energy to Orford before my friend could say anything else. Sheer terror ran across his face as he twisted in pain. He slumped down with a moan, fighting back the tears. Nash called for his extra henchmen from beyond the tombs, the first of whom marched over to pick up Orford, dragging him over the uneven stone floor to dump him at his feet.

"Oh dear, oh dear," he began, laughing before sending another agonising surge through Orford. "Your mother and I correspond regularly, you know, boy." He smiled, sending one more painful blast.

Orford screamed out. I couldn't bear it.

"We can do this all day." Nash laughed again.

"No, please!" I cried. "Stop! You don't need to do this. I'll give you what you want."

He narrowed his eyes.

"Yes, you will." He paused for a moment, his eyes like pools of ink, cold, demonic and void of compassion. He averted his glance from Orford to sneer at me. "Look, my dear," he began. "No hard feelings but you'll never be able to manage your gifts. You've no idea how to use the power it provides to save our people."

"Neither have you," I replied defiantly. "That's why the dragon left you all those years ago. What's to say it won't do the same again?"

Nash's face contorted at my insolence. "Is that what you think? Is this what your father told you?"

I didn't answer.

"Not so confident casting a spell now, are you? Let me guess. The great Hendrick Myerscough has been lying to his long-lost daughter yet again. Will you ever be able to trust him?"

I stood silent, knowing full well his intention was to provoke me and yet, I still found it difficult to redirect my animosity as a sense of bitterness filled me far too quickly. I put my hands together in namaste. I wasn't ready to give up my life that quickly to fuel his monstrous negativity.

"Let me explain," he said, kicking Orford out of the way with a thud. "I'd like your dragon, but I don't *need* your dragon. I need your elemental energy. Dragons are often associated with elemental power which is why they are attracted to ebonoid. It's true, I lost the dragon that came to me as a boy and I'd like it back, but as you know, you can't choose your totems – they choose you. So…if I kill your dragon, it will weaken you, as you did to me last year when you killed my snake. It will make it easier for me to take your spirit and embrace the elemental power that it holds, which is all that I need to rid Magae of Dwellers. Only then will I be able to protect the Magaecian people. Mind you, looking at you now, I can see that's hardly necessary. You're going to be easy to defeat with or without the dragon." He shook his head at me, adding a creepy smile, weird and deranged.

My teeth chattered so much it was impossible to chew my fingernail. I felt the world closing in on me. I could do nothing but remain where I stood.

"Don't look so sad. It's a sacrifice you should be proud to make, Ellery. You might even be remembered as a hero for it."

"The dragon came to me to give me courage. I'm not afraid of you, Nash."

"It's *Mr* Nash," he snapped back at me. He put his hand under his jacket to pull out a tarnished silver dagger with an intricate Celtic knot on the top, then raised it above his head and laughed. "Do you know what this is?"

The blood pumped so loudly in my ears, I barely heard him.

"A Celtic backscratcher?"

"You'll need a sense of humour for what I've got in store for you and your friends."

"Lucky me. I hope you've got balloons and party bags."

"Enough! This is a dagger, used in ancient times for slaying dragons, so they say. It's a priceless heirloom passed down to Sir Farley Fernsby."

"Farley Fernsby…Prickly Bottom, right? Wasn't he friendly with a Nutter?"

"Is this how you want to play?" He bent down to Orford, tugging a clump of his hair to pull his head back, exposing his neck.

"Who shall we start with?" he asked, dragging the dagger near Orford's throat, nicking the side of his neck to produce a crimson bead of blood.

"No! Don't hurt him, please!" I cried out with an outstretched arm. Paralysed by such an overwhelming surge of terror, I thought I might vomit. Orford told me not to think like Nash, but I knew what Nash was thinking. I knew what he'd have to do for his plan to work. It wasn't about making me angry, it was about negative emotions to produce negative energy. He was going to kill all my friends. My resultant distress would produce an excess of negative energy, more than enough to weaken the spirit within me for him to attach successfully to it. He'd won. I'd failed and I was frightened. He was about to destroy me so utterly and completely. I couldn't stop the tears from falling. This, in itself made me weaker but I couldn't stop. I couldn't think of a way to distress him back. He didn't feel love or emotion towards anyone. I'd run out of ideas and plan B was long gone off the plank and a million miles down a black hole with Thomas. Poor Thomas.

For the first time in my life I wished my father were here to save the day like he always did. I'd disobeyed him on a regular basis and now all my friends would pay for it. I hadn't even had a chance to tell him that I loved him. I should have done that. I could have…but I'd chosen not to. Why hadn't I told him? I continued to add to my distress in a hope it would make it easier for Nash to consume me without hurting my friends, but in my heart I knew the truth – I knew he'd make me watch repeatedly as he snuffed out my fat friends one by one. I knew I'd suffer savagely as he broke my heart and destroyed me to the core. Perhaps by then, I would welcome death with open arms.

I squeezed my eyes shut tightly, wet from crying, only too aware that this was to be the end of the line. I waited for my life to flash before my eyes, like it does in the films, but it didn't come. I wasn't really surprised – such a flash only comes at that point in time, those micro-seconds before life is up. I still had to endure a lengthy premiere starring all my friends, who would die a horrible death, before I was allowed to see my own life story. I kept my eyes shut, squeezing more and more tightly, willing it all to be over. Overwhelmed with dread and sheer panic I forced myself to search deep down into my soul for a ray of light in my darkest hour, for just a glimmer of hope. Despite struggling desperately, I couldn't give up now, not until I found that serendipity, a flash of the solution. A flash was all it took. My tongue was intensely tingly. I had to bite onto it to stop myself from dribbling.

"Wait!" I shouted, snapping open my eyes. "Let me persuade you to look at the world from a different perspective. To work on what's good instead of accentuating what's bad."

"Haha! Like your uncle, you will not alter my view."

"But understanding another viewpoint is a sign of strength, not weakness. Why can't you use the anger you feel to motivate instead of to crush and attack? Your revenge is destroying you, it's not saving your people. We want the same thing, don't you see?"

"You will not alter my view!" he yelled.

Nash's obvious desire for revenge meant that my spell didn't work. He was a bully and unable to remove himself from his own opinions to see the side of anyone else. I suppose, deep down, I knew that would be his response. My tongue tingled so much I could barely speak.

"Then let me say goodbye to my friends...please. It's the least you can do," I said.

Nash got up and faced me, lowering the dagger to his side, sending me a single nod as a signal. I knew I had Magae's power. I could almost feel my bones vibrating with her elemental energy. I pushed my hands together in namaste then slowly moved them apart to grab the air in front of me, making a fist in each hand.

"I'm sorry," I cried to my friends. Meanwhile my mind focused on Nash's dagger, still clutched tightly in his hand.

"I love you all," I continued.

Still focused on his hand gripping around the dagger, I drew my fists backwards before flourishing an instant upward cross of my wrists above my head, leaving my body open and exposed. As if an invisible force had seized hold of Nash's hand, tightening the grip on his dagger, I drew him like a magnet, hurtling towards me with such ferocity he had no time to think. He couldn't let go and had no time to stop himself as the momentum carried him forwards to advance like a storm. His arm was outstretched against his will, still gripping the dagger to unavoidably plunge it straight into my chest.

I fell back, the dagger almost embedded up to the hilt. A shockwave of pain burned through my upper body. I gulped for air and collapsed onto the floor.

"NO!" he roared. "NO!" he screeched with an ear-splitting wail, his hot temper practically frying the air within the room.

"I guess this means you know the story of Benvolio and Blaze," I choked. I felt myself smiling. It was ridiculous. I was about to die and yet I was euphoric. I'd got him. I'd actually got him.

Nash's men and my captive friends screamed in agony from the vast ebonoid energy emanating from Nash. It bounced off the walls sending vibrations round the tombs, crumbling stones from the cave to smash everywhere. It was like being in an earthquake. I couldn't focus. I think I was in shock as I struggled with the room that was spinning in front of me.

From Nash's angry temper grew a hideous creature. An enormous wyrm, a Loch Ness demon serpent, savage and brutal as it spat out venomous breath to kill the unfortunate henchmen that happened to block his way. Limbless and wingless with shiny horns on its head and neck, it slithered around screeching and spitting before heading for the tombs. He was going for my friends. I had to stop him but with every breath, a piercing pain ran through my chest. I felt sick. I tried to shapeshift but a wave of pain gripped me so tightly it took my breath away.

The dagger was still in my chest. I grabbed the hilt and with a deep, agonising inhalation, I yanked it out. A dazzling blanket of white and silver spots clouded my vision as I started to black out. I blinked hard to force myself not to. From the corner of my eye, Orford's silhouette limped over to retrieve something from the ground. I think it was my dragon totem stone. He held it in his hand, closed his eyes and shapeshifted. He shapeshifted into a dragon. A magnificent silver dragon that slightly resembled a giant bat mixed in with a lizard. He wrapped his tail around the wyrm to grip it, then threw it away from the tombs.

The wyrm turned and sucked in almost all of the vault's air, causing the air pressure to drop so suddenly my ears popped. As he exhaled, he blew out an inferno so wild it engulfed the vault in a sea of flames.

I looked over to the tombs, soon to be my friends' deathbeds if I didn't do something. I couldn't breathe as I put my hands together in namaste, forcing myself to find my totem dragon, but it wasn't coming. Orford's dragon flew over to the tombs to somehow release Kemp, slicing at his bindings with sharp claws. Before he had time to do the same for the others, he was walloped away by the wyrm's lashing tail, which flung him straight into the wall behind.

I thought Kemp had vanished until I noticed a tiny mouse on top of Letty's tomb, biting away at her bindings. As my friends escaped, running for shelter towards me, Orford sat stunned on the other side of the room, rubbing his head.

"It's okay," said Nyle, who was now beside me. "You need to put pressure on that," he added, unzipping my jacket.

Letty lifted my top and smiled.

"What's so funny?" I rasped.

"Nothing," she said. "How big were you trying to look under there?"

I laughed but stopped suddenly when the pain hit me like an electric shock.

Nash's wyrm threw out a breath of acid towards Orford's dragon which mixed in with the flames, whirling a fiery circle around him. He was trapped.

Nyle stood up, looking weak and skinny from his torturous ordeal. He snatched the bloody dagger from the floor and ran onto the tail of the wyrm like a dragon-slayer, ascending a spiky stairway. He'd almost reached the top with such nimble agility I'm not sure the wyrm was even aware of his presence until the beast raised itself upright, like a massive pillar of evil, its enormous blunt head snapping back to face Nyle. Nyle leaped backwards, then took a blind run, lunging the blade straight into its throat. He removed the dagger and repeatedly stabbed at the wyrm until it thrashed so wildly Nyle could hardly keep his balance. He grabbed one of its grotesque, spiky horns to lever himself up and over onto the wyrm's head. With the dagger held tightly in both hands, he raised it above his head then let out a yell as he rammed it down using all his weight to pass it through the wyrm's crown. The wyrm screamed as it keeled over, convulsing and twitching onto the floor. Nyle tore out the dagger then got to work hacking off the wyrm's head.

"What are you doing?" shouted Letty.

"The only way to kill a dragon, of any sort, is to remove its head or stab it in the heart. I don't think this thing even has a heart so I'm going for the head."

Once detached, the gruesome head lying in a dark pool of blood, Nyle paused to catch his breath. Behind him, as if appearing from thin air, stood Nash, seething and spitting. He smashed past Nyle, knocking him sideways into the treacly gore on the floor, before marching like a soldier on a mission towards me. His pace quickened at an alarming rate, transforming into a run.

"Now, Ellery. Now!" screamed Orford through his smoky prison, the flames edging nearer to him. "Before it's too late! Do it!"

I closed my eyes, knowing that I could attach to Nash's power. It must've been at its weakest. The only chance I'd get. Once I'd attached him to my dying spirit, we would both die.

"Get me to my feet," I said, reaching for Letty's hand.

I stood as upright as I could, which must've been hardly at all, then I let go of her. I held my hands in namaste, followed by a couple of uncomfortable breaths to feel a strange connection as I let my senses go, to be one with Magae. A brilliant white orb floated from me towards Nash, then from Nash towards me, combining into one larger orb of energy. It hovered for a moment between us, then shot through my injured chest, a bolt of pain. I threw back my head in distress, my body rising up in the air, before hurtling backwards with a thump onto the ground. Barely conscious, I could hardly breathe, my mouth so dry, struggling to swallow. I forced myself up, catching a glimpse of Nash. He let out a pathetic squeal, his eyeballs rolling backwards in their sockets as he collapsed like a puppet whose strings had been cut. His life energy had gone and so had he. My knees buckled as everything in front of me spun out of control.

"We've got to help, Orford," gasped Letty. She took out her totem stone from her pocket and closed her eyes. She flew to Orford, a courageous heron flapping over the crackling flames around him. I looked over, searching for Orford but I couldn't see him through the cloudy pea soup of smoke. *Had he been burned alive?* The air was so thick with choking fumes it was virtually impossible to see anything. Cutting through the black haze, a heron flew towards us, carrying a lizard in one webbed foot and a bat in the other, dropping them from a height before landing herself. At least we were all together now. The problem was, if we didn't get out soon, we wouldn't get out at all. We wouldn't be able to breathe. Consumed by the dread of an inevitable end, I stared at the roaring flames in front of me. I held up my hands to shield my face from the heat.

"We've got to get you all out of here," said a deep voice I recognised…but it couldn't be.

"Dad?" I said, turning to cuddle him so tightly round his neck I wasn't sure I'd be able to let him go.

"Thomas has gone," I said, crying. "You need to leave me here. You can't save me now. Just take my friends, please. Don't let anything happen to them."

"No can do, kid."

"I need to tell you something."

"Shhhh."

"I need to tell you that I love you. I should have told you before. I—"

"I know. Tell me later."

My eyelids grew heavy. I blacked out again for a moment.

My father scooped me up, leading the way out of the fiery vault and into an area which turned out to be an underground part of the prison cells. Radella's route had been right after all. We ascended a set of stone stairs to take us to the ground floor and out of the building, but we were forced back by roaring flames. Choking on the smoke, I felt my tongue tingle.

"There's no way through," cried Letty.

My tongue continued to tingle. I guess I had one last chance before I was spent.

"Put me down, Dad," I whispered.

He looked at me strangely but did as I asked.

Holding my chest, I ascended the stairs.

"Ellery, no!"

"I've got this," I said, turning back for just a second before slapping my hands together in namaste. I released them, open to my sides, and focused on the fire. I could do this – fire was one of Magae's elements. As I walked up the stairs, so I moved the flames ahead of me like an invisible force pushing them out of the way. I pushed and I pushed until we'd all got out of the building. I closed my eyes and with all the breath left within me, I embraced my dragon. It came to me like an old friend, filling me with its indomitable spirit and strength. I felt no pain from my wound, only vigour and a sense of worth as my relevance injected a new burst of energy. I inhaled to suck up the ball of flames ahead of me, the burning heat threatening to spontaneously combust me. As I held onto the scorching element, searing pain melting my very core, I twisted round to release a fiery breath like a beast, back to the cell block with a massive blast as it erupted like a volcano, throwing everyone backwards onto the scorched grass as the old building went up like a rocket, sending broken bits of the prison cells to ricochet off in a storm of sharp, splintery debris.

16

AWESOME HUMANS

Sirens blared and paramedics gathered round. I lay dazed and still, incoherent as key workers in fluorescent jackets asked me questions, ripping through my outer garments to get to my stab wound. I was surprised not to be dead yet. Maybe the adrenaline had gone into overdrive. The scene around me seemed to play out in slow motion. Even the noise blurred into one slurry pitch. I tried to speak but my mouth didn't work. Perhaps I was dead after all and having an out-of-body experience.

"We've an air ambulance landing now. It's okay, my love. I'm going to give you something for the pain before we leave," said a lady paramedic.

"I'm not going to make it to the hospital."

"Auch, nonsense. Of course you will, my love. They're going to fly you to Aberdeen. We've no facilities here. Nothing to worry about. We'll take good care of you, I promise."

"Are you the girl's father?" asked the lady, looking upwards as she injected me with something or other.

"Yes. I need to go with her," said Dad.

"Of course, sir. Follow me."

"My friends," I said, sounding drunk. I grabbed Dad's hand from the stretcher as they raised me up.

"They'll be fine. Hakan is here. He'll look after them. I think Ashkii and Radella are handing round hot chocolates. Don't you worry, you brave, brave girl."

A warmth washed over me before everything went black.

***

I opened my eyes which felt so heavy, onto a sterile room with hospital-green walls. It smelled of disinfectant and coffee. My dad snored loudly in a chair beside my bed. I looked down at the big dressing over my wound.

"Can I come in?" said Aab, peeking through the door and waking Dad with a jolt.

I nodded with a smile. As I tried to sit up, a burning pain spread across my chest.

"Easy does it," said Dad, fluffing up my pillows.

"Why don't you get a coffee or a chocolate, Hendrick? You've been here all night."

"Thanks, Aab. Can I get you anything?"

"No, I'm fine. What time is Nell arriving?"

"Mum's coming?"

"Of course she's coming. She'll be here this afternoon," replied Dad as he shut the door on his way out.

"I'm so glad to see you still breathing, Ellery," said Aab,

sitting at the edge of the bed.

"Aab? Why didn't I die?"

"The answer is multifactorial," he replied.

"What do you mean, sir?"

"It is for many reasons, Ellery. One reason, I think you'll agree, is sheer luck. One might say it is because you have the heart of a dragon, and that is very difficult to pierce. And then, of course, you managed to acquire the life force of another ebonoid which would have given you extra protection. Also, it appears you had some spare socks within your T-shirt...in case your feet got wet?" He chuckled. "Anyway, this acted well as a buffer so that the dagger was less able to penetrate as far as it could have if the socks had not been there."

"I see," I said, cringing, trying to think of something to change the subject as quickly as possible away from my boob enhancements.

"Aab? Why didn't my father tell me the story of Benvolio and Blaze?"

Aab raised his thick silvery-grey eyebrows as a smile crept across his face. "I would think that is obvious, Ellery. He knew you might well do exactly what you did because he knows his daughter to be courageous and selfless. He did not want to lose you. He was right, as a father, not to tell you."

"But you knew I might get myself killed."

"I'm afraid so. But I knew also that Nash would succeed in killing you if you did not have all the options at hand."

"I see. I always thought I was here to bring back balance to Magae, to somehow change the way Nash saw the world, but he was never going to change, was he?"

"I'm afraid not. But I think you are right about bringing back balance to Magae. Your job was not to change the world, but instead to stop Nash from removing the world of the chance to at least try. You succeeded in doing that. That's balance. You see, alone you can make a change, together we make a difference. Nash was never going to make a difference acting alone. We have to work together."

"Aab, one more thing, sir…"

"Yes?"

"Orford turned into a dragon: a cross between a lizard and a bat."

Aab nodded with a smile. "I thought he might. He truly was your guide, was he not?"

"Yes, I guess he was."

"You are lucky to have such friendship and love among your contemporaries. I'm not sure I've ever experienced such courage among younglings before. We are all very proud to call ourselves your teachers."

The door flung open, bringing a flurry of friends to my bed.

"Don't tire her out too much," said Aab. "She needs her rest." He smiled then left the room.

"You were bloody amazing," said Orford, hopping in on crutches, his face a shade of blue, green and yellow from all the bruises.

"So were you," I replied.

I noticed Nyle look down at the floor.

"So were you, Nyle," I added, prompting him to grin.

"Bloody awesome, mate," continued Orford, which was unexpected. "The way you ran up the wyrm like nothing…and then you were like…straight for the jugular… ahhhhh!…" He was re-enacting the scene with one of his crutches as the dagger.

"And then you did that flying leap onto its head and jabbed it in, full throttle…totally Hawk!

You were like Captain wyrm-slayer!"

I noticed Letty and Kemp were holding hands as they laughed at Orford's description.

"Ellery," said Kemp, edging towards me. "I'm sorry about all those things I said to you."

"Don't be. It's already forgotten."

"Can I come in?" said Mr Mitchell, at the door with Ash by his side, looking slightly aghast at the number of visitors in the room. "You were all incredibly brave, kids, including Thomas, whose bravery will not go unmentioned or forgotten."

A silence covered the room like a blanket as we each took a moment to remember our fat friend, a true Musketeer – kind, loyal and generous.

"Well done to Ashkii too," added Mitchell, patting him on the back.

"I didn't do anything."

"Yes, you did, young man. You set off the fire alarm at *The Palace*."

Ash turned scarlet.

"He never did!" said Letty.

"It was genius. The quickest way to get everyone's attention. It enabled Mr Myerscough to reach you before it was too late and it meant we could call for help – paramedics, police and firemen."

"Mr Mitchell, sir?" I said.

"Yes."

"I thought shapeshifting was something we did in our head – not in the real world."

"Yes, Ellery. It is."

"Then why were we not our totems all of the time? I mean, Nyle wasn't his dog when he ran up the wyrm, he was himself…"

"Ah. I see," said Mitchell. "This is not unheard of. Your totems are here to assist you and guide you in the best way possible, whatever the circumstances may require. When Nyle ran up the wyrm, he still had his dog totem attributes but within a new totem…"

"What do you mean, sir?" asked Nyle.

"I mean, you shapeshifted into a *Nyle* totem. A human form. A mixed totem. A human form with a dog's heart. It was more suitable under the circumstances, seeing as dogs are not that great holding a dagger. You exhibited your loyalty, trust and protection so typical of a dog totem. You see, although we see humans as only occupying the physical world, this is not completely true. It's unusual but your animal totem can also be a human. After all, humans are animals too," he said, with a smile.

"Sir?"

"Yes, Ellery."

"Has the dragon left me now?"

"Totems often come and go when, and as, you need them. Your dragon gave you the strength and courage you needed. If you require such attributes again, it will return to you, although I think perhaps you will *always* have the heart of a dragon. I don't think that will ever leave you."

"Thank you, sir."

He paused. "You're an unusual group of kids. I think we may still have a future on Magae with a generation like you."

"Good Lord!" gasped a nurse, walking into the room with my meds. "Far too many visitors, I'm afraid. You're a popular lass, aren't you? I'm sorry, but you all need to leave now. Come on," she said with a chuckle as she ushered everyone out.

"Orford, dear," she added as she grabbed his crutches from Nyle who was playing with them, "you can sit in here with Ellery for ten minutes until your grandmother comes to collect you. You're not meant to be putting any weight on that knee, remember?"

An abrupt silence filled the room on everyone's mass exodus. Orford hopped over to my bed and sat beside me.

"Do you really think he'd have done it?"

"What?" I asked.

"Nash. Do you really think he'd have killed me?"

I shrugged. "I think he intended to kill all of you."

There was an awkward pause.

"I read *The Catastrophe of Callistus*, by the way," said Orford.

I raised my eyebrows.

"What you did…it was bloody brave."

I shrugged again.

Orford brought his face nearer to mine, gazing into my eyes as he brought his lips within the same breathing space as my own. I felt sharp palpitations through my chest as our lips met. I closed my eyes and let him kiss me.

A loud knock on the door forced us to break apart.

"Your grandmother's here, dear," said the nurse.

A mischievous look crossed Orford's face as we both broke into a laugh.

Half-term came and went while I recuperated at home with my mum. Not long after that, school closed completely. Not just my school but all schools around the world. A deadly virus had infected every nation, requiring quarantines and lockdowns. Dad said it was just the type of stunt Nash would have thought up, letting out a virus to stop people travelling to work and closing all polluting factories to clear the air for Magae. Mum said it was Magae's way of telling us that we needed to pull our socks up and show her more respect. *One last chance*, kind of thing. Mrs Huckabee's logical explanation was that we'd destroyed so many natural habitats we'd now encroached on and come into contact with animals far more closely than we should have, exposing ourselves to viruses that we wouldn't otherwise have done.

I wasn't sure what to think. I guess I knew it was human impact behind this pandemic and possibly behind pandemics to come if we, as a species, didn't change the destructive relationship we had with Magae. I knew that our devastating loss of biodiversity was also our fault. Our disconnection from Magae, destroying her natural balance, was only going to lead to disaster.

One thing I had learned was that one person alone couldn't save us. Mankind had to work together. Maybe this virus would actually work to rebalance the planet, saving us from a much greater disaster. We could still fix this and we had to, while we still had time. We were all in this together, no matter whose fault it was. We had to concentrate on the stuff we *could* do and not on the stuff we could not. We needed to stop using our rivers and estuaries like sinks to dump industrial pollution. We needed to plant more trees, clean up our cities, waste less, consume less. We needed to produce affordable food without expanding further into forests. We needed to stop degrading our soils. We needed better laws to make positive changes in favour of saving Magae's biodiversity. We needed to do a *lot*! But Magae, or Mother Earth, if you prefer, would bounce back – she always did, given the chance. I only hoped she'd give *us* the chance to prove we were worthy inhabitants to remain on her planet. Perhaps we'd have to reverse roles so that children taught their parents.

We needed to be positive. I knew this more than anyone. So long as we had hope, we'd have a future. Besides, we were awesome humans! We were totally Hawk!

17

CHEF MACBRENNAN'S COMFORT FOOD SPELL

SMOKY BEAN CASSEROLE

(a favourite at Quinton House)

Serves about 6
Preparation time: 20 minutes
Cooking time: 30 minutes

Ingredients

2 tablespoons olive oil
1 large onion, finely chopped
1 clove garlic, crushed
1 teaspoon smoked paprika
1 x 400g tin chopped tomatoes/or equivalent fresh tomatoes
2 tablespoons tomato purée

1 tablespoon vegan Worcestershire sauce (optional, but Chef MacBrennan says it gives it that extra yum factor!)

1 dessert spoon coconut sugar

1 teaspoon herbs de Provence

100ml red wine/vegetable stock

1 x 400g tin butter beans, drained and rinsed under cold water

1 x 400g tin chickpeas, drained and rinsed under cold water

1 x 400g tin haricot beans, drained and rinsed under cold water (Chef MacBrennan uses a lot of beans! You can reduce the amount to half if you prefer)

Freshly ground salt and pepper

A little water to thin the sauce if required

The spell

In a large frying pan, heat the oil and gently fry the onion and garlic for a couple of minutes until softened.

Add the smoked paprika and stir.

Stir in the tomatoes, tomato purée, Worcestershire sauce, coconut sugar and herbs de Provence.

Add the wine or stock and leave to bubble up, then simmer with a lid, remembering to stir from time to time.

Add the beans and continue cooking for about ten minutes or until it thickens.

Season with salt and pepper.

Serve with whole-grain rice or sourdough bread or maybe a wholemeal rustic loaf.

Delicious!

Warning: do not mix with wyrms!

ACKNOWLEDGEMENTS

'm not going to list all the many books I've read or the incredible people who have given me the knowledge that I needed to truly understand our planet's dilemma. The information I've acquired in recent years has sent me down many a dark path over lost forests, over-production of meat, mistreatment of cattle and other animals, over-fishing in our oceans and injustice on so many levels. I'd like instead to leave a list of some of the amazing charities and organisations, working around the clock to make our world a better place with a sustainable future.

The World Wide Fund for Nature (WWF) (wwf.org.uk) Their mission is to "create a world where people and wildlife can thrive together."

Greenpeace International (greenpeace.com) Greenpeace is a big supporter of ocean conservation and forest preservation as well as protecting endangered species and supporting the prevention of climate change.

The National Geographic Society (nationalgeographic. com)

You might have read their magazines or seen some of their TV documentaries. They provide a bird's eye view into why it's important to save the planet.

Friends of the Earth (friendsoftheearth.uk)

They describe themselves as "part of an international community, dedicated to protecting the natural world and the well-being of everyone in it".

The Royal Society for the Protection of Birds (rspb. org.uk)

This organisation recognises the plight of our planet, particularly our dwindling bird populations.

The Climate Coalition (theclimatecoalition.org)

The Climate Coalition describes itself as "the UK's largest group of people dedicated to action against climate change"

OTHER TITLES IN THE SERIES

BOOK 1:
CLASH OF THE TOTEMS
AND THE LOST MAGAECIANS

"This is an action packed adventure and coming-of-age story with an inventive and unique twist, 'Clash of the Totems and the Lost Magaecians' is set up to be the start of an interesting new series."
LOVEREADING4KIDS

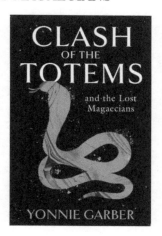

The start of this audacious adventure where Ellery must uncover the secrets of her past in order to understand her destiny to protect humanity's future

Sign up for my occasional newsletter and other releases
www.yonniegarber.com

ABOUT THE AUTHOR

Yonnie Garber is a foot doctor (podiatrist) turned word-charmer (author). Her attention has inevitably progressed from ailments of feet to where those feet tread.

An ardent member of the WWF she is passionate about increasing awareness of human impact on our environment.

As a mother of five and a grandmother of two, storytelling has always played a big part in her life, so Yonnie has combined both her passions to mix moral principles with epic tales of adventure.

She believes that a change is growing in people's minds and hearts, spreading rapidly towards a greater respect for the Earth, so that we may all create an optimistic future.

Yonnie Garber is a member of scbwi (the Society of Children's Book Writers and Illustrators) and ALLi (the Alliance of Independent Authors).